The World Pool
A Literary Variety

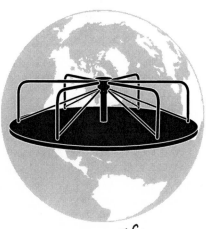

FIC

ROBERT LEO HEILMAN

A SYLPH MAID BOOK

Sylph Maid Books
P.O. Box 932
Myrtle Creek, Oregon U.S.A.
97457
(541) 863-5069

ISBN 978-0-9908686-3-7 (Paperback)
ISBN 978-0-9908686-4-4 (ebook: Kindle edition)
ISBN 978-0-9908686-5-1 (eBook: ePub edition)

Cover and interior design and composition by Judy Waller;
cover and interior illustrations by Judy and John Waller.
www.johnandjudywaller.com

Printed in the United States of America

Literature is the embodiment of our thought.

It travels over endless miles, sweeping all obstructions aside; it spans innumerable years acting as a bridge.

Looking down, it bequeaths patterns to the future; gazing up, it contemplates the examples of the ancients.

It preserves the way of Wen and Wu about to crumble; it propagates good behavior, never to perish.

No realm is too far for it to reach; no thought is too subtle for it to comprehend.

It is the equal of clouds and rain in yielding sweet moisture; it is like spirits and ghosts in effecting metamorphoses.

It inscribes bronze and marble, to make virtue known; it breathes through flutes and strings, and is always new.

—Lu Ji, *Wen fu* (286 A.D.)

*F*or James Ross Kelly
My steely eyed editor and my friend

Acknowledgments

The following pieces first appeared in these publications: "Sailors on Horseback," "Lloyd O. Nelson: Wake Island POW," "By the Skin of our Teeth," and "The Improbable Adventures of Hathaway Jones" in *The Table Rock Sentinel,* Medford, OR; "Fuji and the War on Young Men" in *West Wind Review #10,* Ashland, OR; "Of Flower Power and the War With the Newts" in *The Central Valley Times,* Grants Pass, OR; "Dialoguing With Eric" in *Northwest Magazine, The Sunday Oregonian,* Portland, OR; "One Thousand Times a Day" in *High Country News,* Paonia, CO; and "Embracing Opal Whiteley" in *Oregon Quarterly,* Eugene, OR.

Contents

Introduction

Variety is the very spice of life,
That gives it all its flavor.
—William Cowper, *The Task II*

$\mathcal{D}$ear Reader,

I think about you often while sitting here with a flickering cursor winking at me and the hours rolling on as the black lines of symbols representing words fill the screen for you. It is an odd compulsion, this desire to write and publish what I've written. It is entirely irrational and, were it not for pleasing you, would not be worth the doing.

This book that lies open here before you is a gift from me to you. As with any gift, the giver hopes you enjoy it, that you may find some small measure of pleasure in reading it, that it might teach you something new or perhaps remind you of things forgotten, that you will find me companionable as I lead you through this little literary variety show.

Here you will find essays, vignettes, histories and short stories that I have written over the past thirty years. Some were done on assignment for magazines and newspapers, others as pieces for book and broadcast projects that never saw print. They have sat on my computer's hard drive, unseen and unread for too long.

Books, stories, poems, essays and columns all live only when being read. They live inside you, in your imagination. It seemed a shame to leave them hidden from sight when they could, perhaps, live for a while with you.

This world is a great big place and filled with many places, times, people and things. There is such variety in our lives, in the natural world, in the people we live among and in our shared human history that it seems a shame to separate these elements of our great swirling world as though harm might come unless they are kept separated in their respective fields.

Welcome to the World Pool,

Robert Leo Heilman
Myrtle Creek, Oregon
April 2016

Prologue—The World Pool

For Richard Paul Heilman

*H*e sits at a picnic table and doesn't speak. He smiles but he is too happy to talk about it. Words could only make his joy seem smaller, because when you get down to it, the really important things can never be said right.

Around the tables, heavy with potato salad, cold cuts, pretzels, soda and punch and beer, the clan is gathered. A family of families, cousins, aunts and uncles, nephews and nieces, grandparents, brothers and sisters, mothers and fathers and in-laws, kin every one of them, tied together by all the accidents of birth, marriage and death, in the caring conspiracy that is a family.

Their voices come to him as music. The low ironic tones of the men, the busy talk of the women, the dry thoughtful cadences of the old, the rapid high pitched chatter and laughter and shrieking of children, the wailing and burbling of babies flows through him not as words but like a familiar song. He knows what's being said without listening to the words, knows what will be before it happens because some things don't change.

He watches the children playing on the merry-go-round and remembers the whirling sensation, the outward pull on straining arms and the blurring background as they clung to the bars, seeming to be still while all the world spun.

The Whirl Pool they called it. "Help! I'm caught in the whirl pool!" they'd shout, but he was very small then and called it The World Pool, because the world was spinning crazily and only they sat unmoving, unchanging, clinging on against the force that wanted to fling them outward, scattering the dizzy brothers and sisters and cousins to the far places of the earth.

He remembers it all so clearly and wonders at the strangeness of passing time that brought him here to his father's place among the men at the table, watching the children play as his dad must have watched.

When he was small everything had seemed so permanent. A patch of lawn was all the world; a sunny day all time. He had been caught up in the pool of the world never guessing that the motion of the great circle whirling past only made it seem like everyone stayed still.

It had happened so slowly, the changes went unnoticed in the day-to-day running around, the whirling merry-go-round of a family caught in the world pool.

A Freeway Runs Through It

$\mathcal{I}$ dreamed of rain the other night. The land was dry, the pasture grass yellowing, the leaves on the forest floor crinkly, and the duff beneath the leaves had turned to a fine dusty powder. Then the rain came and the hidden life of the soil stirred joyfully all around me. I felt a great calm and pleasure, as if my own body was the land. I too was being restored by the cooling drops and turning green and limber where drought had left me brittle and desiccated.

The next morning, low clouds sat over our little southern Oregon valley. The hot, dry May haying weather of the past three weeks gave way to cool and damp. That evening it rained.

I've lived here in this valley for forty years now, for more than half of my life, and now the landscape of my dreams is divided. Sometimes I have Oregon dreams set in a world of salmon, sword fern, cedar and fir, logging roads, fields and pastures; sometimes I have California dreams of city streets or of dry brown hills, dreams from my childhood in Los Angeles.

There used to be a hilltop world there, an island of chaparral rising above the sea of streets and houses. It was a small place really, a hundred acres or so of abandoned sheep range. This patch of sage brush, yucca, cactus, yerba buena and manzanita clinging to the pale-yellow decomposed granite slopes was our sanctuary, and that of remnant wildlife—deer, coyote, skunk and rabbits.

A dirt road ran along on a ridge up "G" Hill to a radio transmission tower. Just below the tower a huge outcropping, "G" Rock, hung bulging from the hillside like an oak gall on a branch. From atop the rock my brothers and friends and I could look out across the paved basins of the city to see other wild islands in the chaparral archipelago, stretching off into the smoggy distance.

The rock was a destination, a place to arrive at and to eat lunch from our paper sack of peanut butter and jelly sandwiches. From up above, the city below seemed as dwarfed as we felt ourselves to be when we walked its streets. Up on the rock we became disdainful giants watching the self-important scurrying of the ants below. Before long, there would always come the uncomfortable feeling that the enormous boulder we perched atop was about to come loose from the hill and roll off like a ball, down to the houses below, carrying us with it. At times, I could feel the forward motion of the aggregate monolith and felt myself rolling forward and downward. It was a good place to sit but no place to play.

From the top of "G" Hill two ridges stretched out like arms and between them was a folded draw. Here, with the hillsides concealing the cityscape, was our playing ground. Hidden by the draw we could at last assume our true dimensions, neither dwarves nor giants, but the exact size of our imagination.

We were at an age when the geography of our imagination was our true world and this little fold in the hills was our true home, where we could cast aside our pretend identities of home and school and walk the earth as our real selves, as explorers, scientists, soldiers, gold miners and cowboys. We traveled a familiar and mysterious terrain where each live oak, boulder and shaded hollow beneath a manzanita was named and had its ghosts and its history.

A seasonal creek ran through it in the spring. A narrow, curving path ran along the tiny creek bed. It was a running-path, a ribbon of pale earth etched by canvas-shoed feet, with wide, swooping curves that crossed and re-crossed the creek bed, swinging high up on the canted banks. Walking on it was tiring and difficult, but to run it was to fly effortlessly as a disembodied spirit.

The rising tide of the city buried this little draw long ago, when I was in the fourth grade. Leathery-skinned men with bulldozers came. The hill top was flattened and the draw was filled and the rivers and jungles and deserts and mountains of my childhood made way for the Glen-Eagle Estates. Later, during my high school days, a freeway was built and an eight-lane strip of concrete cut through the neighborhood and through the hillside below "G" Rock as straight and unswerving and precise as an exercise in Euclidean geometry.

Yet, fifty-something years later and eight hundred miles away, I run that path still. In my dreams there is no sadness over the loss, only the joy of running. Awake, I know that tens of thousands of cars and trucks drive over my childhood every day. Their drivers' thoughts hurry ahead to their destinations, unmindful of where they are, hurtling over the buried world of my memories and my dreams.

In talking with my son I've learned that although we both sometimes fly with our dream-bodies and use the same flight techniques, his is a different dreamscape than mine. There are no power poles and electric lines for him to carefully avoid as there are in mine, and no streets lined with buildings. His spirit floats over a Northwest world of forested mountains and whitewater rivers and cow pastures.

My older dreams, the primal ones which are so deeply a part of me, have urban dreamscapes which he's never dreamt about. I suppose that my own father's most familiar dreams took place among the grasslands, wheat fields and solitary buttes of his childhood North Dakota, though his adult body lay asleep in Southern California, surrounded by the City of Angels.

Surely, a dream so common that I've never met anybody who hasn't flown while asleep must be an ancient one as well as a fundamental one from earliest childhood. My grandfather then, probably dreamed of a dirt-lane village on the Nogai Steppe of Ukraine while sleeping through North Dakota blizzards.

Dreams are so portentous and yet silly, that it's

hard to say just what they mean. I sometimes dream that I'm writing, juggling paragraphs and sentences and weighing words. I awake to wonder whether I was composing in my sleep or simply dreaming about the act of writing, my daily work, just as I've dreamt of shingling roofs, pulling lumber in a mill and doing farm chores.

The phantom world of sleep and the waking world coexist, but in complex, unfathomable ways, and no one really knows how they affect each other. Still, there must be some connection between the fond hopes and the nightmares of our fear in the daily world and the surreal lands of sleep.

Mine must be the only generation in the family to dream of a childhood city. My son is thirty-four now. He's left his father's house, the only home he'd ever known. Like so many of our valley's young men and women, he has chosen to live in a large city and perhaps the line of fathers and sons in our family will have a fifth generation growing up far from their father's childhood home and the second to be raised in a city.

One hundred and four years after our family came to this continent, our dreams remain the divided dreams of immigrants. We dream of both the world of now and of a world that is lost. I'll never know what it is to have but one landscape, the same waking and dreaming. Nor will I ever know what it is to dream only of the same lands that my ancestors before me dreamed of and dreamed in. I cannot go there, where perhaps the old ones remain in their dream worlds, and my son will never know mine.

It was a fine thing to dream of rain and the relief of a drought broken at last, to feel no difference between the rain, the earth, your body and the joy that moves through each and all. It was made finer still when the rains did come just as in the dream. Yet I'm haunted by the notion that it would be finest to have shared it.

Rough and Tumble

$\mathcal{D}$ad must have gotten the 8mm movie camera as a gift on his thirty-third birthday, November 5, 1952. There's one older film in the cardboard box, 1947 in grainy black and white, the stucco and Spanish tile house on Gardenside Lane, the Big Boys, fair-haired little Jimmy, Billy, Dickie and Charley out on the lawn, running through the sprinkler. With four sons in six years, my mother was a little worried that she might never have more children, might never have a daughter.

Go ahead. Laugh.

It seems silly to me and to your granny too. But what did she know? She was twenty-six years old back then, not a whole lot older than you, unable to see into the future any more than you can now. How could she, that woman with curly red hair standing on that sunny post-war lawn, know that the next eleven years would bring five more children? Five years later, in the fullness of time, Dad got a movie camera of his own and shot his second roll of film, in color this time, on November 17, 1952, my sister Patty's third birthday. She stands behind a cake-laden table in the front yard of the house on

Alessandro Street while a choreographed troupe of my brothers and a half-dozen arm-swinging neighborhood kids marches single-file up the sidewalk, past the telephone pole, into the driveway and then in circles around the table. I was there too, a baby just a few days shy of nine months old, clinging to the table and reaching for the birthday cake.

Memory sometimes plays tricks on me. I cannot remember that birthday party, or many of the other bits and pieces of our lives that my father captured on film. Yet, the memory of seeing the films when I was a little goomer has gotten mixed up in my mind with the genuine memories of that small house by the Los Angeles River where I shared an attic bed with two of my brothers.

It was a rough and tumble world, full of bumps and tears and exuberance. We grew up as a noisy, churning, scampering and squalling, barefooted bunch. Looking back, it seems as though it was a world almost without parents, as though we raised each other in a semi-feral childish Frogtown Neverland like Peter Pan's Lost Boys. In that world, my sister Patty was my Wendy, always watching out for me, letting me tag along.

On my way home from North Dakota a few years back, I stopped in Glendive, Montana to visit Aunt Maggie, my dad's sister. I wanted to hear stories about my grandpa Lorenz and among other things she told me a story she'd heard from him about a visit to our house in Los Angeles back in the early 1950s.

"One of the kids was just a baby, still in diapers,

couldn't hardly walk yet, and Pa saw him open up some drawers on the kitchen counter and he started climbing up to get a baby bottle," she told me. "Well, you know, Pa never could stand to see kids going hungry. On the farm we always had neighbor kids over for dinner and supper and we'd just set a few extra plates and feed 'em. Some of those kids didn't have much to eat at home, you know, back in the Thirties what with the Hard Times and all. Anyway, he said he felt so sorry for that baby and the little booger was so determined to get that bottle and so Pa got up and got it for him and gave it to him. He laughed about that for years, used to tell that story all the time."

Though I hadn't seen my dad's films in thirty years, I realized that that baby was me. Cap Heilman, like his father, loved little children and since I was the baby at the time when he got his camera, there's more baby film of me than any of my younger brothers. I suppose my big brothers must have put me up to it, getting me to walk and to climb after my bottle before I was a year old. My dad must have thought it was amusing too since he filmed two of my acrobatic baby bottle quests, one of which is in the kitchen with me opening drawers on my way up to the counter top, just as Aunt Maggie described it.

I'm glad she told me that story among the dozen or so I heard on that visit. Knowing now what I've learned about Grandpa Lorenz's hard childhood, it all fits together. It comforts me now in my middle age to know that I earned my tough old grandfather's pity, admiration and kindness back before I learned to speak. I feel lucky to have an almost-memory made up of two short bits of old home movie film and my Aunt's little story.

I guess it's hard for you, an only child, to understand fully just how deeply I'm touched by these old flickering images. My family must seem like a confusion of names. Well, it confuses me too sometimes, when I look back on it. Mom and Dad and us nine kids were just a small part of who we were.

"An extended family" it's called nowadays, though no one back then thought of it as such. It was just our daily lives, filled with uncles and aunts, some of whom were actually my parents' cousins and great-uncles and great-aunts or simply friends of theirs who were our godparents. There were cousins by the dozens too, forty-two of Grandpa Lorenz's grandchildren and thirty more of J.P. Holzemer's. You could get lost in such a crowd, sometimes painfully so, but sometimes delightfully lost and never lost for long. There was always somebody there when you needed them, and always somebody there when you wanted no one. Kinship imposes a necessary kindness, binds us in ways that demand more of us than the ties of friendship do.

Because he was usually the one holding the camera, there's very little footage of my dad. What I remember about him shooting film is a row of bright lights that hurt my eyes. It was like having the sun appear in your living room, held aloft by an indistinct looming form whose cyborg face was half-human and half machine. One of the rare times when he stood on the other side of the camera was in what must have been 1954.

The occasion was my first haircut, administered by my Godfather and namesake, "Uncle" Bob Zimmerman, and it's obvious that I am indebted to my older brothers, Dick and, especially, Hop, for this silent 8mm glimpse of my dad. Uncle Bob was my father's friend, a film stage carpenter who told childish jokes and performed sleight-of-hand tricks. He had the knack for making children feel like they were neither more nor less as important and worthy of love as anyone else.

Bob Zimmerman was also an amateur barber and he must have saved my father a good deal of money over the years by bringing his electric clippers and fine-toothed comb along when he and "Aunt" Pete dropped by. My Godfather, wearing a Hawaiian Aloha shirt in the film, kneels on the floor of the old house on Alessandro Street, talking to me, a two-year-old with a head fringed in wispy blonde baby-hair ringlets. Hoppy and Dick hover about while Uncle Bob shows me the hand shears, comb and black electric clipper. He's smiling and joking and explaining to me what he's about to do.

I'm smiling as he cajoles me, at least until it's time to put me in a chair. Hoppy, eager to be part of something memorable, grabs me by the chest and lifts me from the floor. Choked by my overly energetic brother, I struggle and burst into tears. There's a break in the action, probably, knowing my dad, long enough to spank poor Hoppy, and when the film continues, Dad is holding me while "Uncle" Bob clips my curly blonde locks.

Forty-something years later, with "Uncle" Bob, my father and my brothers, Dick and Hop, all dead from their heart attacks, I nearly cried again on seeing the film.

Both Cap Heilman and Bob Zimmerman had a great fondness for children, and, in my own way, I've deliberately tried to emulate my dad's whimsy and my godfather's easy gregariousness whenever I'm around a child. This is how the dead we loved live on, providing a little bit of their personality for those who remember to pass on to those who never met them.

Sailors on Horseback

$\mathcal{O}$n the Tuesday morning of September 21, 1841, Passed Midshipman Henry Eld, USN, paused along the trail atop Rooster Rock overlooking the site where the city of Myrtle Creek, Oregon, sits today. Three years into a journey which would carry him around the world, he'd already been to some of the world's most remote and beautiful places, Rio de Janeiro, Antarctica, Tahiti, Samoa, Australia, Fiji and Hawaii. Still, the scene struck him as unusually beautiful.

"Here is one of the prettiest views we have seen in the country," he noted in his journal, "from a nearly perpendicular height of a couple of hundred feet, you look down upon the limpid Umpqua winding its way gracefully among the mountains in deathlike silence, not a living thing to animate the beautiful scene, not even a canoe is skimming on its waters, the inhabitants the few remaining are scooted in the dells and glens, lying wait and meditating deep & dark vengeance against the white man, who by disease have depopulated the country & who they wish to make accountable for their crimes."

He decided to make a sketch of the scene, and as the rest of his party—an odd collection of U.S. Navy sailors, marines and officers, scientists, mountain men, Indian guides and settlers—left him behind, the uneasy sense of loneliness must have grown stronger, for he added the figure of an Indian, dressed in a cedar bark coat, to the foreground. Engrossed in his work, Eld lingered too long.

"At this place while I was attempting to sketch a little of the topography of the country as we went along, the party left me, & before I was aware of it, I had completely lost my way, crossing over a creek that the party had gone over, could find no trail although I made two or three miles each way, but nothing could I see or hear of them in any direction & began to feel the horror of being alone in an unknown country, and the inhabitants only wanting the opportunity to cut off any white that they could, and dare attack; ..."

His fears were soon increased when he met up with a group of Indians. "They made motions to me to go back where the white men had gone, but taking out my compass and found it was running nearly North & feeling sure that our party could not have taken that path, and that they were designedly leading me out of the way, put spurs to my horse made a dash directly thro the place they had issued from and continued in a SW direction & the took the first opportunity of getting to the South and thro a valley, with the hope that I should strike into the trail..."

He finally found the trail again, and, after missing a pistol shot at a scroungy looking wolf, "the poorest creature I think I ever saw," he caught up with the party near the Riddle/Tri City interchange on Interstate 5 and by one o'clock was camped near present-day Canyonville.

Eld was in southern Oregon as a cartographer for the United States Exploring Expedition, an unprecedented scientific research project carried out by the federal government through the U.S. Navy. The project had been hatched nearly twenty years before under the administration of John Quincy Adams but ran into immediate problems from opponents who questioned the constitutionality and usefulness of government support for science.

National pride (and the hope of finding new sealing islands and whaling grounds) finally carried the day when the French and British both announced plans for Antarctic exploration. Very much like the space race of our century, the American people wanted to be the first to either reach the South Pole or discover the unseen continent which geographers theorized must exist somewhere below the Antarctic Circle as a counter-balance to the lands to the north.

In addition to the primary goal of breaching the ice barrier, the expedition was instructed to survey the South Pacific, searching for reported islands of uncertain location, finding new ones, and mapping the uncharted waters of known places such as the Fiji archipelago.

Finally, the expedition was to survey the Pacific Northwest to provide the government with information useful for negotiations with the British aimed at settling what would come to called the "Fifty-four forty or fight!" issue over the boundary between the United States and Canada.

After years of controversy not only with a stingy Congress but also between the Navy and the scientific community, a squadron of six ships set sail on August 18, 1838, from the Navy yards at Norfolk, Virginia with 346 men under the command of Lt. Charles Wilkes.

The next two years brought many dangers. The expedition's schooner *Peacock* was nearly crushed against the ice barrier in Antarctica. Two members were murdered by natives in the Fiji Islands where the crew of the *Vincennes* also witnessed cannibalism. "It inough to make a mans blood run cold to think of sutch," the expedition's taxidermist, John W. W. Dyes noted in his journal.

Still, the expedition accomplished much, dotting the uncharted coast of Antarctica with American names—Wilkes Land, Eld's Peak, Point Emmons, Peacock Bay, Cape Hudson and Ringgold's Knoll—taken from members of the expedition, and producing America's first accurate charts of the South Seas. The scientists collected tens of thousands of specimens of little-known and new species as well as recording important ethnographic information on the Polynesian cultures which were already in serious decline under pressure from contact with *haole* whalers and missionaries.

After contributing to the decline of the culture they studied by burning a village in reprisal for the deaths of their companions, the expedition finished their three months' stay in the "Cannibal Isles" and sailed north to the Sandwich Islands, arriving in

Honolulu in August, 1840. Here the ships were refitted and the crews enjoyed a prolonged shore leave among the seven bowling alleys, numerous grog shops and "Loos Ladyes of Pleasure" who, despite the efforts of the missionaries, would often visit the ships when the officers and scientists were ashore. Not surprisingly, many of the marines and sailors either jumped ship here or refused to re-enlist when their terms expired in November.

Wilkes tried to keep his men busy over the winter months overhauling the ships and exploring Hawaii and other North Pacific islands, but the missionaries no doubt breathed a sigh of relief when the expedition left for Puget Sound in April, 1841.

Two of their ships, the *Peacock* and *Flying Fish,* which were out on a cruise to Wake Island and other spots until June, left Honolulu on the Fourth of July with orders to enter and survey the Columbia River while the larger ships were in Washington. They arrived off the Columbia bar on the morning of July 17, where the *Peacock* ran aground on a sandbar that afternoon. Caught between the river's strong flow and a heavy ocean swell, the ship broke up the following morning, by which time the crew was huddled around a drift-wood fire on shore at Cape Disappointment.

Lt. George F. Emmons, the ship's commander who'd ridden her down the ways at her launching, wrote in his journal, "Thus I have witnessed the beginning and the end of the Peacock, having been launched in her at New York in 1828, and wrecked in her on the Columbia Bar in 1841... And there is some consolation in knowing that after the many narrow risks she has run this cruise—that her fate has been prolonged until reaching her native shore."

Emmons secured the services of a one-eyed Indian pilot named George and they rowed out to the smaller *Flying Fish* which, guided by the pilot, crossed the bar and picked up the survivors and took them to a camp near Astoria.

It was August by the time they were reunited with the rest of the expedition. Lt. Wilkes purchased, after some haggling, the *Thomas W. Perkins,* a Baltimore brig, to replace the lost *Peacock* and rechristened her the *Oregon.* He was helped considerably in buying the ship by Dr. John McLoughlin, the Hudson Bay Company's factor, who agreed to purchase the brig's cargo, rather than having Wilkes' stranded sailors on his hands "getting into quarrels with the natives, and bringing the whole country into trouble."

McLaughlin also lent horses and mules and gave advice for an overland expedition from Ft. Vancouver to San Francisco, which Wilkes ordered. Lt. Emmons was picked to lead the party and was given a group consisting of Midshipman Henry Eld, surveyor; Titian Ramsay Peale, naturalist; Alfred T. Agate, artist; William Brackenridge and William Rich, botanists; geologist James Dwight Dana; John S. Whittle, surgeon; Midshipman George M. Colvocoresses; and two servants, all guarded by Marine Sgt. Albert Stearns with a detachment of two sailors and three marines.

They bought horses and mules from the Hudson's Bay Company, got advice from mountain man Tom McKay, and hired six "half-breeds and Canadians" and an Iroquois Indian named Ignass to guide them.

News of the party's trip got around and soon three families of settlers and four unaccompanied men wanting to move to California joined up with them. When they finally left Ft. Vancouver on September 7, 1841, the group had grown to thirty-nine people, including four women and eight children, carried on the backs of seventy-six horses and mules.

The party entered southern Oregon on September 15 and the following day camped along Elk Creek. Lt. Emmons decided to visit Ft. Umpqua, the Hudson's Bay Company post, near present-day Elkton.

"Therefore leaving Mr. Eld in charge, with directions to wait my return, I continued on accompanied by Mr. Agate and taking along with me Sergt. Sterns, Doughty & Boileau [Hudson's Bay Co. trapper Joseph Beaulieu], the latter as guide, being the only one of the party who knew the way."

"After a forced & fatiguing jaunt of about 21 miles over the worst country I have ever yet traveled, up & down a succession of steep craggy mountains… we finally arrived upon N. shore of the Umpqua River about 8:30 P.M. …"

"Finding no canoes on this side of the river, fired several guns to attract the attention of those in the Fort, whose position owing to the fog, could only be determined by a light and the howling of many dogs. The flash of the first gun produced a screech from the opposite shore and those that followed appeared to add considerable to the excitement, and it was only after frequent hails that we obtained an answer. Mr. Gangere

[Jean Baptiste Gagnier], the Canadian in charge, being acquainted with Boileau finally recognized his voice and dispatched two Indians with canoes in which we were finally ferried across…"

They found themselves in a small stockade "defended by 5 men, 2 women and 9 dogs" which was surrounded by "many Indians sculking about among the bushes" who, Gagnier explained, "had lately threatened to attack him & burn his fort. Their hostility arising toward the Co. and Whites generally from their losses by small pox which was first introduced among them by the H.B. Co.'s Party under Michael [Michel LaFramboise] or [Tom] McKay…"

Over a late supper of "a bad cup of tea sweetened with dirty sugar, with an accompaniment of coarse but wholesome bread and dirty butter…" the French-Canadian trapper filled them in on the local Indians, "adding that I could learn but little from their outward appearance (little suspecting probably that I had had intercourse with even worse people for the last 3 years) but that he knew their character well & that they were 'terrible Mauvais Savage'."

The Navy lieutenant and the Hudson's Bay Company agent sat up late, Emmons learning all he could about possible ambush sites to be avoided up ahead and dickering for horses and supplies. He also tried to find out as much as possible about the Company's business in the area, noting the defenses of the fort which he later sketched.

"Mr. G. made us a bed out of blankets upon his stall & bidding us good night, locked the door, put the key in his pocket, and retired to the adjoining house."

"Up at daylight and were let out—fleas were troublesome during the night. A thick fog still hanging over the fort. Got an early breakfast—Mr. Agate improving the interim in sketching a group of Indians. Were made acquainted with a custom of the dogs & hogs about the fort too disgusting to mention."

Emmons and the others returned to the main group that evening to find Gagnier's warning strengthened by a visit from Indians who "had given such account of the character & intentions of the Indians to the south of us that many of the party evinced an uneasiness which I took some pains to dispel."

They set out the following day, September 18, for what proved to be a very uncomfortable journey through southern Oregon. Several members became ill with "chills and fever" including Alfred Agate and Emmons himself.

They had arrived during the traditional field burning season, when the local Indians set grass fires to improve feeding conditions for deer and elk as well as to gather tar weed seeds for food. The skies were overcast with smoke, the charred ground tore at their horses' unshod feet, and there was little forage for the mules and horses. To their military minds it seemed that the Indians were engaged in a scorched-earth campaign designed to impede and weaken the party prior to ambush.

In the afternoon of September 20, just south of modern Roseburg, they came upon two grizzly bears, the smaller of which scampered out of the way. The larger one reared up and faced them and was shot in the lungs by Titian Peale, but managed to get away with two more bullets in him. "Among all the animals I have ever seen, I do not think that I have ever witnessed so formidable an enemy," Emmons noted, "and regretted very much at the time that it was impracticable for me to preserve the skin of the largest (which far exceeded any in size that I have ever witnessed in museums) for our National Museum that I trust is to be."

Though the bear's hide eluded him, Emmons' hope for a national museum was fulfilled a few years later when Congress, faced with the necessity of housing and cataloguing the tons of specimens and thousands of artifacts gathered by the U.S. Exploring Expedition, voted to use the bequest of James Smithson to establish the Smithsonian.

They camped that night along Clark's Branch at Round Prairie and made it to Canyonville the next day. On the twenty-second they started up the rugged trail along Canyon Creek, a mountain pass which later gained notoriety as the "Dread Canyon of the Umpqua," by all accounts the worst portion of the whole Applegate Trail.

William Brackenridge, the party's chief botanist, described it in his journal: "Began to ascend the Mountains at 8 A.M. . . . the path being narrow through masses of brush and loose rocks, so that we had to follow each other, forming a line at least one mile in length . . ."

"Indeed," Henry Eld noted, "this has been the most difficult and fatigueing day of any we have yet experienced, the mountains so steep in some places that some of our animals fell backwards in attempting to climb, their loads becoming top heavy & completely losing their balance, turn heels over head."

In addition to the usual hazards of the trail, Lt. Emmons was faced with other problems. "...The mountain had lately been set on fire by the Indians, doubtless to obstruct us (The boughs were in many bad places artfully tied together from opposite sides of the path, so as to entrap the riders & sweep them from the horses backs, found a cutlass of considerable service to us in this particular.) and larger trees had fallen across our path so that we were in many instances obliged to cut our way through or around them. And the mountain path was always more or less obstructed by broken limbs and brush which was now tough and blackened by the fire... we were unable to escape many hard rubs and scratches which I fancy made us look more like a band [of] devils on horse back than any thing human."

Brackenridge too thought the party looked odd after their exertions: "...the woods lately been on fire and before we got over wer as black and uncristian like as so many Negroes from the coast of Africa..."

It was a day of accidents. At least three pack horses tumbled from the trail. Someone's rifle fired off unexpectedly when the hammer caught on some brush. Lt. Emmons was swept from his horse by a snare. Titian Ramsay Peale lost his journal and some equipment when a pack tore open.

After a smoke-darkened day of "...groping my way along half blindfolded," it must have been with a great sense of relief that Lt. Emmons and his party "...reached a beautiful little valley" unharmed and settled down for a good night's rest along Cow Creek near modern-day Azalea. However, Emmons watched as one last accident unfolded to cap off the day.

"During the night I was wakened by the cry of No! No! and upon looking from under my tent disc'd that one of the horses had become entangled in the adjoining tent stretchers & after kicking furiously for some time finally pulled the whole fabric down upon the marines who were the principal inmates, & who took no further trouble to extricate themselves until daylight."

The next day, September 23, the party halted to rest the horses while Peale backtracked in search of his missing equipment. They were in a new country now, and set about describing the plants and trees and animals—soap plant, sugar pine, and Blacktail deer—not seen farther north.

They found themselves among the "Rogues or Rascals" whose language they could not understand. Here, midway in their journey, the party was anxious to push on. The horses and mules were suffering from a lack of forage on the burnt grasslands and from the accidents and exertions on the trail. Several of the government expedition members were suffering from Tertian Fever, brought on by malaria which they had picked up in the tropics. The skies were overcast with smoke haze and the Indian Summer weather held in the 90–100 degree range during the day, plunging to near 30 at night.

They were also nearing what they feared would be the most dangerous portion of the trip, the trail through the Rogue River Valley along which they would pass through three different sites of past ambushes, some of which their guides themselves had survived. "We rarely send parties of less than 60 armed men along that route..." Dr. McLaughlin had warned Emmons before they set out. The Overland Party had only twenty-seven armed men.

On the afternoon of the twenty-fifth, Ignass, the Iroquois guide, was attacked while away from the group skinning a deer that he'd shot. He answered arrows with rifle fire and escaped on horseback. That night, while camped along the Rogue, the guards chased off some intruders from camp and found a woven basket full of cooked roots near one of the tents.

The following day they camped downriver from Gold Hill on the site where a party of mountain men had been attacked by the Takelma, who killed three of the trappers. The trappers however had evidently "…killed a number of the Indians whose bones we found bleaching in the Sun." The party found that a band of about fifty Takelma were encamped across the river. They spent an uneasy night among the bones where "…the yells of Indians close by us were constant untill midnight."

They set out on the morning of the twenty-seventh expecting to be attacked at Rocky Point where the trail was hemmed in by the river on one side and a rocky slope on the other. Peale saw "…Indians on the opposite side of the river running, apparently with the object of cutting off our passage across a rocky promontory covered with brush; the place was favorable to an ambuscade, and as there was no way to avoid it, we prepared for hostilities…"

Lt. Emmons led a group of fifteen skirmishers ahead on foot leaving the other men behind to bring up the horses and guard the women and children. It was a tense few hours but, other than hurling taunts from the

other side of the river, the Indians left the party unmolested. "…And twas well for them as ther were some
deadly Shots among the party who wanted nothing
better than to get a sight of one of the rascals," Brackenridge wrote in his journal.

After following the Rogue River beyond Rocky
Point for two hours they "…struck off southwardly
through a pass in the mountains, and reached extensive
plains, where we saw three mounted Indians who fled
on our approach," according to Peale.

Despite the excitement, naturalist Peale noted a
small herd of antelope in the Bear Creek Valley and
commented on the large numbers of hares and "long
hedges constructed of thorny brush" built by the
Indians to trap them in drives. Here too the grasslands
were burnt providing "but poor provender for our
horses, some of them gave out on the march but overtook us at the camp…" The horses were slowly starving,
becoming weaker by the day.

Midshipman Colvocoresses became delirious with
fever the next day and was unable to ride. Faced with the
prospect of halting in what Peale described as "…the
most dangerous part of the country—where the natives
are most murderous and avowedly hostile…" Emmons
chose to push on, leaving the malaria patient behind in
the care of surgeon Whittle, Peale and three others, who
brought him along "…in very short and easy stages
untill we overtook Mr. Emmons at night."

On the way up Bear Creek (which Emmons called
"Beaver Creek" for the many beaver dams) Peale, Whittle and the others "passed a sulpherous spring" and saw
"a squaw who was so busy setting fire to the prairie and

mountian ravines that she seemed to disregard us; her dress was a mantle of antelope or deer skin, and a cup shaped cap, made of rushes. She had a funnel shaped basket, which they all carry to collect roots and seeds in."

The following day, September 29, they ascended the "Boundary Mountains" along the trail which led them to Pilot Rock which Lt. Wilkes designated "Emmons's Peak" in his narrative of the expedition "as a memorial of the value of his services in conducting it safely through this hostile country."

"The sick were able to proceed again this morning, but Mr. Colvocoressis soon became worse as the sun gained power; which obliged us to make several halts before reaching the bloody pass... Country everywhere overrun by fire," Peale wrote.

"Passed the dreaded 'bloody pass' without difficulty and without seeing an Indian—only a few of their tracks, and after surmounting a high mountian ridge, a view of singular granduer was spread before us; on our right the mounts. were burning, and sent up immense masses of smoke; on our left was the snow summits of Mount Chasty—extensive plaines were in front of us... we had a hot and thirsty ride of about 20 miles to the Tchasty river, near to which on a small branch, we halted for the night—bread and tea only for supper."

Despite the hardships and danger, their two-week journey through southern Oregon yielded a good deal of scientific and military information—maps, lists and descriptions of flora and fauna, and ethnographic notes describing the remote *terra incognita* of Oregon—all useful at the time to the fledgling republic of the United States of America and invaluable today in understanding our past.

Over the mountains in the Mexican province of California, the going was easier with more forage for the horses and friendlier Indians. On October 19, the party reached New Helvetia on the American River, John Sutter's huge private empire. Captain Sutter welcomed the expedition and, talking "a little largely," showed them around his truly impressive holdings. For all his talk, the Swiss immigrant no doubt listened well when geologist James Dwight Dana mentioned that he'd seen "the strongest proof and signs of gold" upriver near Mt. Shasta.

Sutter supplied Emmons with a boat to carry the sick 120 miles downriver to San Francisco Bay where they rejoined their ships on October 23. Henry Eld brought the rest of the party overland five days later, paid off the guides and sold the broken-down horses, which Emmons noted wore "a look that plainly told of their sorrows," for $5.00 each.

Casus Belli

It's the spring of 1964, fifteen months before the Watts Riot and we're Boy Scouts on a weekend camping trip to Cabrillo Beach.

It's the uniform, of course, that's cool and everybody is a Scout, all of us certifiably Courteous, Kind, Obedient, Cheerful, Thrifty, Brave, Clean and (above all) Reverent. Half of us are altar boys. We wear our black and white kerchiefs (the colors of St. Dominic, the old Inquisitor) with the white side on our left—purity next to our hearts. We marched in review at the cathedral and the archbishop himself blessed us adolescent Christian paramilitary soldiers, Troop 9.

We're more boys than scouts, caught in that desperate limbo between childhood and manhood, still playing army, but telling half-understood dirty jokes and sneaking cigarettes, masturbating quietly in our sleeping bags and worrying about maybe being queer.

We have only each other. The adults are enemies, the nuns at school are no longer saintly but just weird old women, and the girls have changed. And no one understands—not even us.

We are all afraid of our own selves and of each other. Any two of us get along quite well; we form friendships as tight as lovers. But, wherever three or more are gathered, we turn on each other, alert for the slightest sign of any failing to be cool and, finding it, attack the victim like a flock of pecking hens. The cruelest of us are the coolest.

It's morning on the kelpy beach. Later, we'll search the white chalk cliff for fossil fish, splitting the soft diatomaceous earth clods with butter knives. But it is morning, the dads are back at camp, pumping the tanks of Coleman stoves or sleeping off side-pocket whiskey-flask stupors. For the moment there's just us, Troop 9, in blue jeans and khaki uniform blouses, out on the beach, standing around on the wet sand and eyeing them—another troop down for the weekend.

They are watching us, hanging together, a loose clump of boys. We're looking back and nobody is smiling. They're all black kids. We're all more-or-less white—O'Malley, Lugo, Montoya, Szalabal, Heilman. We know all the jokes: "Oz who?"; "Oz yo' new nay-buh!"; "A nigger, a chink and a greaser…"; "Fo' a nickel I will." The jokes are about all we know though. They never come to our part of the city. They wouldn't dare to walk the sidewalks of Eagle Rock. Our parents would never sell a house to their parents.

And maybe that's not a big deal, at first. Maybe they're just not us is all and it would have happened anyway, them in uniform and us in uniform and all those John Wayne movies and our dads with their old scrapbooks and medals from the war and the uncles whom we know only from photographs because they never returned from the Philippines or Belgium or Italy and the Commies will certainly be on our better-dead-than-Red shores someday soon and we're prepared.

We are prepared.

Maybe we start it; maybe they do. It seems like mutual consent, inevitable. Everyone scooping up handfuls of wet sand, flinging them in their faces, blacks at whites, whites at blacks, two sides that quickly merge in a jumbled shouting mass for a five-minute eternity. There's a fear-filled fierceness in their eyes, perhaps in ours too, but there is no time to think or notice. We all scoop, fling, spin our backs, too late, as the stinging sand strikes our faces and necks and gets in our eyes.

And suddenly, it's over. We've been driven back from the shore toward camp, muttering, "Fuckin' niggers, fuckin' niggers …"

Fuji and the War on Young Men

*F*uji wanted to know what I did. "You are student?" he asked. We were standing beside I-40 in Albuquerque in the spring of 1970. I wasn't a student anymore. Two months earlier I had dropped out of high school. There was a war going on in those days and I was living at a commune founded by the Up Against the Wall Motherfuckers. But how do you explain that to a young Japanese hitchhiker who barely speaks English?

"No, I live in a commune," I told him, pointing at the Sandia mountains whose broken, jagged strata rose in the distance. "It's a farm. You know. I'm a farmer."

"Fah mah?"

"Yeah, you know—a farmer. Make things grow?"

He brought out a multilingual dictionary with its red plastic cover. I searched through seven different languages but there was no translation of the word there in any of them.

I looked up from the book. The young man with an unpronounceable name grinned brightly back. He looked like some all-American teenager out of Archie Comics. I wondered what he thought, how he saw

America, here on a freeway on-ramp in the timeless pastel landscape of the West. How could I explain my own arrival here a few minutes earlier, with thirty-eight cents in my pocket and an eight hundred-mile journey to Los Angeles ahead? What's the Japanese word for hippie?

"You are not student?" he asked.

"No, I'm a…" A what? It's hard enough to label yourself in the best of times. Most people give their occupational title, but I didn't have a job and I had a deep distrust of labels. Like Alice, I knew who I used to be, but I'd been through several changes since then. "…a farmer. We grow food, you know, corn and beans and stuff."

He was clearly puzzled. "You go to university?"

Only to panhandle or to score. What could I tell him that would be both true and understandable? Truth was everything. Whatever it was it had to be devoid of pretense. A would-be saint? An acid-head? A poet? An outlaw? There was truth enough in all of these. But I saw myself as a gentleman farmer, someone who cultivated plants and whose desire was simply to be left alone and to let the world go to hell on its own.

There was a lull in the traffic. I squatted down and pantomimed the act of planting a seed, choosing a piece of gravel and carefully burying and watering it. I made chopping motions with an invisible hoe. My hands traced the growth of the seed into a plant and then the harvesting and eating. I looked up eagerly, hoping to see the light of understanding in his face. He had a deeply puzzled and vaguely embarrassed look on his face.

"Shit. You don't understand?"

"No. You are student?"

"Yeah … I'm a student."

"I am student too. I go to university in Japan."

A State Police patrol car cruised by and I tightened reflexively. It didn't stop though. New Mexico cops were relatively easy to deal with anyway, not like in L.A. where a cop would, as often as not, approach me with a drawn pistol just to run a computer ID check. I don't think that New Mexico even had a police computer system in those days.

It was a sort of game—Blue Meanies vs. the Flower Children—though the consequences were quite serious. We accepted our roles: after all, there was a war going on and this was the America of Richard J. Daly and Abby Hoffman. You could tell by looking at the uniform which side one was on. Everyone knew, except for Fuji.

Fuji didn't notice the cops. He stood, arm uplifted in an exaggerated hitchhiker pose, like a stick figure beside the highway, while a small school of cars streamed past and we failed to hook one.

It's easy to feel insignificant when standing beside an Interstate trying to catch a ride. The cars and trucks pass by in chromed and enameled self-sufficiency and as the hours go by you feel yourself blending in with the rest of the landscape, becoming a weathered roadside fixture. You can fight it for a while, reading the scrawled messages on traffic signs, tossing pebbles, scratching out designs in the dirt. Eventually, you lose your sense of self-proportion; half-conscious, you swell to mountain size and shrink to mouse dimensions. Finally, you draw numbed indifference about yourself like a cloak.

But hitchhiking with Fuji made the world all new.

I saw with his eyes the strangeness of the familiar desert, felt the intensity of blue sky, wondered at the distant, convoluted mountains, smelled the cleansing sagebrush. Even the wide gray bands of pavement reaching for infinity seemed charged with meaning.

"It is very beautiful," he said. "America is very beautiful."

I agreed.

Beauty abounded everywhere, if you had the eyes to see it. It could be seen in the smallest of things—a scrap of weathered wood, an old shoe. In quiet moments the powerful simplicity of things, the subtle nobility inherent in them would reach me. At times I could see it in everything and everyone, no matter what the scale—an essential something that eluded definition but which could be experienced as beauty. It had become, to me, the proof-mark of reality and the basis for my morality.

Fuji too, it seemed, understood the importance of beauty. We would travel together then, sharing the journey, tasting the sweetness of the ancient landscape of the Southwest, exulting in mountains and mesas and limitless sky. That one word, "beautiful," was all the language we would need.

It's been twenty years now since that spring, and it was one of many road trips I made hitchhiking all over America as bereft of money as I was of purpose. It must have taken us several rides from start to finish, but I can only recall the first and last of them.

What is it about memory that retains beginnings

and endings while the middle gets lost? Is it that the midst of things is unknowable mystery? Or are we simply busy doing and don't notice what goes on around us until it is over, when we find ourselves comparing the start and finish and wondering what happened to all the steps between?

Just before we caught our first ride a jet flew overhead, to Fuji's delight.

"F-104, very good plane!" he beamed. He told me that he lived near an American Air Force base back home in Japan and rattled off the names of various aircraft frequenting the place. "U.S. Air Force number 1! Very good planes."

His enthusiasm for military technology set me back. Didn't he know there was a war going on? I'd made my own decision a month before by not registering for the draft, a crime punishable by five years in prison. I feared prison, and expected to end up there eventually, since every encounter with the police was a potential arrest for violating the Selective Service laws.

How could my companion praise the machinery of death and destruction? Had he forgotten our fathers' war? How could he? I grew up killing Japs with toy guns and avocado hand grenades.

Still, his enthusiasm had been genuine and innocent. He had meant his praise as a compliment of sorts, a tribute to my country's ability to build fast, sophisticated planes. He must not have known that he was traveling through a nation in which the issue of peace had divided us into armed camps. He couldn't have known that the war in Asia had its counterpart here at home or that the twin wars were really just two equally ugly fronts in one war, the war on young men.

I have heard that the death rate for American men aged eighteen to twenty-five was higher in the late 1960s than it was during WWII. I can believe it. In those days, if the Viet Cong or the cops didn't get you, life on the streets, drugs, random violence, suicide or car accidents could.

Two weeks earlier, on this same highway, a trucker had tried to run me over, steering his double-trailer semi ten feet onto the road shoulder to the spot where I'd stood moments before. It had happened at dusk when the highway was empty. Later that summer, outside of Denver, a beer bottle, tossed from a passing pickup exploded against a traffic sign three feet behind me and about a foot over my head. On a freeway on-ramp in San Bernardino a middle-aged man driving a bobtail truck gave me the finger, his face contorted in a mask of sheer hatred. Wherever I went that summer, from Oregon to Florida, one message was made clear: my kind weren't wanted.

A battered beige Ford station wagon pulled over for us and we grabbed our packs and ran up the road-side without discussing war and peace. The driver was a fat middle-aged Chicano, and a Navaho woman sat in the passenger seat. He was a social worker giving her a ride to Gallup. The woman spoke Navaho and Spanish but no English. The driver spoke English, Spanish and Navaho. He was delighted to have a Japanese student on board and kept asking him how to say different phrases in Japanese. He tuned in the Navaho radio station but Fuji didn't understand a word of it although Navaho sounds a lot like Japanese to me.

In a roadside rest area on the way to Gallup I asked Fuji where he would be staying when we got to L.A. He didn't have any place to stay there, so I told him he could flop with me at a friend's house once we hit town.

He accepted and thanked me. "You have beautiful heart," he told me. There's no higher compliment.

The last ride came just before dark, in that time when colors lose their value and the world is seen in silhouette. We were standing in front of an abandoned gas station on the outskirts of Holbrook or maybe Winslow, Arizona when a semi pulled over for us and we clambered up into the high cab with the driver.

Fuji crawled into the sleeper behind the seats and I sat in the passenger seat. The driver was tired and needed somebody to talk to so that he could stay awake. I was approaching exhaustion myself but since Fuji couldn't speak enough English to keep the conversation going, I sat up with the driver while my partner slept and we bounced through the night.

The trucker said that he was heading to San Bernardino and would be arriving there around sunup, providing we both stayed awake. The truck wasn't a very comfortable ride but it beat sleeping with the scorpions and rattlesnakes by the roadside.

We climbed the long grade up to Flagstaff, the trucker constantly shifting his gears and adjusting his lights with toggle switches on the dashboard. It was my first ride in a semi and I felt like I'd made the grade as an official hitchhiker.

Between Williams and Kingman the truck developed an ominous clunking, something wrong in the drivetrain somewhere. The driver pulled over and looked around beneath the truck with a flashlight. It was a moonless, starry night and the headlights cast long shadows that were swallowed up in the darkened desert.

Fuji sat up in the sleeper space and rubbed his eyes. He'd slept through the bumping and clunking of the truck but the stillness awakened him. "We are in California?" he asked.

"No, Arizona. The truck's broke down."

"Broke down?"

"Yeah, it's broken. It don't work."

"Ah, broken. We walk?"

"Maybe. I don't know, we'll see."

We sat in the uncertain glow of the cab's dash lights, our ride a mote in the dark as lone as any star. Hunger and exhaustion were catching up to me. My mind filled the blackness with bright speckled patterns moving in drunken waltz time.

The driver returned from his inspection. "Damn U-joint's going out. We'll wing it into Kingman. I'll call in and see if the company wants to have it fixed there or if we can try and make it to San Berdoo."

"We stay," I told my road partner. There was more I wanted to tell him, about the odds on getting arrested in Kingman. I'd heard all about Kingman. I should have warned Fuji but there was the language barrier and more importantly, there was too much to explain that wouldn't make sense to him, a traveler in a country whose problems he didn't understand.

"Well, I hope we keep going," I told the driver.

"Oh well, ain't nothing we can do now. It's up to the dispatcher. If he says 'park 'er' I gotta park 'er."

It was a long, slow ride in the heaving semi into

Kingman. Fuji went back to sleep and the driver and I didn't talk much, both of us busy with our own worries.

Kingman was a strip town, a string of neon signs three or four miles long. The driver pulled into a graveled lot next to a corrugated metal repair shop and made a phone call from a pay booth. Fuji woke up and I explained to him that we might go on with the truck or we might have to walk out of town.

The truck stayed; we walked. We walked less than a half mile, our backpacks patting us reassuringly, before a squad car pulled up alongside us with the blue lights flashing. A big blonde cop with an American flag patch on his sleeve got out to question us. He checked our ID, amused by Fuji's passport's seals and incomprehensible writing, and suspicious about my lack of a draft card. I told him I'd lost it and was on my way to L.A. to get a new one.

"I bet you burned it," he replied. "Well, you're coming with me." And then he turned to Fuji, "You can go." He brought out his handcuffs and locked my wrists together behind my back.

It took Fuji a moment to realize what was happening. Confusion gave way to dismay on his face and he tried to ask why I was being arrested.

"My friend, he…"

"You go," the cop told him. "He's coming with me."

"I'm sorry man, I got to go," I told him. "It's OK." What could I say? I was sure that I was on my way to five years in prison. I worried though that he would think he'd been traveling with an escaped convict.

"Go on. Get out of here. He's going to jail. You go," the cop said over his shoulder as he hustled me into the back seat. I turned to look at Fuji as the cop closed the door. He was standing there looking shocked and confused and sad and lonely.

"Goodbye," I said, feeling sorrier for him than I did for myself. He still didn't believe what was happening. I could see that in his eyes. He came over to the window and he wanted to say something, but the words weren't there. "I'm sorry," I said. "Really. Goodbye."

Lloyd O. Nelson: Wake Island POW

*L*loyd Nelson sits in the kitchen of his home near Roseburg, Oregon, recalling things long past, history now, written up in articles and books, but alive in his memory and still affecting his life every day.

He's a big man whose body has rounded with his seventy-two years. His blonde hair has gone gray and balding, his large hands and his face are lined by the passing of time, but his voice, his blue eyes and expressive face show that he's lively, energetic and sharp. A lifelong resident of Douglas County, he reaches back fifty years to talk about 1941.

You know, it's hard to remember just what went on during the battle. It was dark out and the surf was so loud and there was just so much going on so fast. You was so busy you didn't have time to think—you just did it. And then later on you try to sort it all out.

The war in Europe dominated the news during the winter of 1940–41. There was also growing speculation concerning a Pacific war with the Japanese as America reluctantly and belatedly prepared for war. But it all seemed a bit remote from everyday life in southern Oregon.

Congress had approved a $7,500,000 appropriation in 1940 for the fortification of five Pacific Islands—Johnston, Palmyra, Samoa, Midway and Wake—as advance bases for defense of the western Pacific. Pacific Naval Air Bases, a consortium of construction companies, including Morrison-Knudsen Company of Boise, Idaho, was awarded the contracts.

Morrison-Knudsen was responsible for building a naval base and airfield on Wake Island, a tiny coral atoll consisting of three low-lying islands, Peale, Wilkes and Wake, enclosing a lagoon. It was the easternmost of the five island bases, located just 1,700 miles from Japan and only 620 miles north of a major Japanese naval base on Kwajalein Atoll.

Wake Island, that wasn't even on the map when you looked for it. They always said it was in the South Pacific. And if I'd known beforehand it was right next to all the military bases of the Japanese and what the world situation was—I'd've probably took another guess at it.

But once you're out there, if you go to work for a big construction company on a project and you turn around and go home, they won't think about hiring you again you know.

When the first construction crew reached Wake on January 8, 1941, the only structures on the island were a hotel and support buildings belonging to Pan American Airways which used the spot as a layover and refueling stop for their weekly China Clipper service between Hawaii and the Philippines.

Work began immediately at a fast pace. But the long hours, tropical weather, and isolation took its toll.

They had a heck of a time getting people on the islands doing defense work. There was more leaving the islands than coming on during the first part of the construction. So they went on a bonus and their food was terrific. They had to have something to keep the men, otherwise they'd just come out, take a look at it and come back home again.

The consortium began recruiting workers to replace those who'd left. In February, 1941, a "Help Wanted" ad appeared in the *Grants Pass Courier* and word of it trickled north to Douglas County where twenty-two-year-old Lloyd Nelson had been working for seven years as a salesman and delivery man for Umpqua Dairy in Roseburg.

I had a good friend of mine that knew about it and said it was good money and everything—plus adventure, so I went with a bunch of the guys. There were twelve of us from Douglas County that went out there.

A chartered bus picked the men up in Roseburg and brought them down to Grants Pass where they joined sixty others. On April 29, the bus left for San Francisco where they boarded the Matson liner *Lurline* for a first-class voyage to Los Angeles, and then to Honolulu where they transferred to a cargo ship that carried them on to Wake Island.

That ticket was worth $125. That's what it cost the contractors. You talk about living like kings!

I sailed under the Golden Gate Bridge on May first, 1941, which was my birthday. I was twenty-three years old then. I come underneath that same bridge, I think it was October the eighth, '45.

Nelson spent the seven months following his arrival working eight- to twelve-hour days, seven days a week. Because of the frenzied pace of the construction he only had three days off.

I worked in a lumber yard for awhile and in a ware-house, the machine shop, and finally got a job being a drag-line oiler, helping the operator. They had us working on a crane, putting up steel buildings and when we had most of that done they put us out on Wilkes Island digging a deep channel through there so the submarines could come in to the lagoon and refuel. That's where I done all my fighting.

The first detachment of U.S. Marines, 173 enlisted men and five officers, arrived on August 19. By Saturday, December 6, two days before the surprise attack on Pearl Harbor (Wake Island lies east of the International Dateline), the atoll held 1,146 civilian construction workers and sixty Pan Am employees as well as 469 marines, sixty-eight sailors, and six Army Air Corps radiomen under the command of Commander Winfield Scott Cunningham, USN.

The construction project was running ahead of schedule. An airstrip had been built but work was still underway on protective revetments, support buildings and fueling services for the twelve Grumman Wildcat F4F-3 fighter-bombers on the island. Six five-inch naval guns, taken from WWI battleships, twelve three-inch anti-aircraft guns, eighteen .50 caliber machine guns and thirty .30 caliber machine guns were in place but most of the artillery lacked essential range-finding and altitude-control equipment.

The marines, under command of Major James P. S. Devereux, USMC, were too few to man all the guns. But more were expected in the months ahead and with the guns finally in place they held a drill to test the communications system and the gun crews for the first time. The drill proved successful and the marines were rewarded with Saturday afternoon and Sunday off.

Word of the break spread to the construction crews and Morrison-Knudsen's superintendent, Dan Teters, declared a holiday. The workers, marines, sailors, and soldiers spent that Sunday writing letters, swimming, fishing, playing cards and softball. Shortwave radio sets played big band swing tunes. A Pan Am Clipper arrived in the afternoon bringing mail. The outdoor movie theater in the workers camp was filled that night.

At 6:50 A.M. the next morning, December 8, an Army Air Corps radioman on Wake picked up a message from Hickham Field in Honolulu. Pearl Harbor was under attack.

There was no radar installation on Wake and the booming of surf on the coral reef surrounding the island prevented the use of listening devices to pick up the sound of approaching aircraft. The twelve-plane squadron of Wildcat fighter-bombers was divided into three patrols of four airplanes each. One patrol at a time was kept aloft patrolling while the remaining eight were serviced and readied.

Dan Teters met with Commander Cunningham and Major Devereux to put his construction crew to work, helping man the gun batteries, moving supplies and ammunition, and preparing shelters and defensive works for the expected invasion of the island. There were not enough rifles, pistols and helmets to arm all of the military personnel should a Japanese force actually land on the island, and with the US Navy's Pacific Fleet lying shattered at Pearl Harbor, the likelihood of evacuation or the arrival of relief forces was slim.

We's stuck; we was up the creek. All we had to do was fight. There was nothing else for us, no guns to go around or nothing else. They was just helpless. I didn't have any gun either, except on the last day I had hand grenades. But you can't fight the military with hand grenades and rocks you know.

The sky was overcast that day and at 11:58 A.M. a Japanese squadron of thirty-six bombers emerged from a rain squall a half mile off shore. They were already overhead and dropping bombs before Wake Island's untried guns were fired for the first time.

We was going off shift and heading back to camp in a flatbed truck when the planes come in. We thought they was American planes but then they started dropping bombs. So we all hid as best we could until it was over.

There was a lot of guys hurt and so I started helping the corpsmen find them and move them over to the hospital. We loaded them up on flatbed trucks 'cause that's all we had. It was a bumpy ride for them but we couldn't do nothing else.

The raid lasted twelve minutes and left about fifty men dead and fifty more wounded. Seven of the eight Wildcats on the ground were destroyed and the eighth heavily damaged. A 25,000-gallon aviation-fuel tank exploded. The airstrip support buildings were destroyed but precision bombing had left the landing strip itself almost untouched. Both the military and civilian camps were hit as well as Pan Am's hotel on Peale Island.

The bombers returned the following day, December 9, concentrating on the airfield and the workers' camp. Though construction workers had painted a large red cross with a white background on the hospital's roof, the building, filled with wounded personnel, was bombed.

That red cross was just a target for them, helped them aim better was all it did.

It was noticed that Japanese reconnaissance planes accompanied each bomber squadron, circling overhead to take photographs for the next raid. A decision was made to move the island's gun batteries every night and put up mock guns in their former places. One-hundred-man construction crews worked all night under blackout conditions moving the eight-ton guns, filling sand bags and digging new emplacements and then caught an hour or two of sleep in the morning before the daily bombings.

We used to take 4x4s, 6x6s and line them up, try to

put a little brush on them. Hell, all they'd be was lumber you know. They'd see that and YERROMMM!

Ol' Charlie Mallor and I, we built a dugout under a tree but they come and bomb us and strafe us pretty close you know. He says, "Well, by gosh, maybe they took a picture of that too. We better move." We moved our dugout someplace else and it got hit that next day. But we was just doing one jump ahead. There's where laziness don't pay.

Nelson was assigned to Battery "F" on Wilkes Island, four three-inch anti-aircraft guns and a searchlight under command of Gunner Clarence B. McKinstry. Lloyd operated the searchlight and helped the gunners.

On Wednesday the tenth a bomb fell on a storage building on Wilkes containing 125 tons of TNT.

There was a lot of dynamite and that whole island just shook. We was in a dugout which was probably only a foot below the level ground you know. You couldn't dig in very easy—not like sand or anything.

Well, it just cleaned all the brush off the island. It looked like No-man's Land. All the leaves and everything else was just all torn off—just the heavy limbs and stuff left.

Fortunately, only one man was killed and four wounded in the explosion.

At 3:00 A.M. the following morning a Japanese fleet was sighted off the coast of Wake. Destroyer Squadron 6, consisting of three cruisers, eight destroyers, two troop transports and two submarines under the command of Rear Admiral Sadamichi Kajioka had arrived with an invasion force of 450 soldiers. Orders were sent out to all the gun positions on the atoll to hold their fire in the hopes of luring the ships within range of the five-inch guns.

That night, night of the tenth and the morning of the eleventh, they shelled the islands and then we didn't return fire. So when they circled the island, shelled it—then they thought they had us whipped, see? So then they started to come in real close. A big destroyer came through and then they had us open fire. They was one or two shells and the thing went SHUSST! They was under water; hit it just a perfect spot.

Then they took off and hauled-ass back to their military bases. 'Cause we hit quite a few other ships too. When we hit that big destroyer they thought we had big ten-inch guns on the island. So when they did capture us they was raising hell, "Where's the ten-inch guns?" you know. It was only five-inch guns.

When the destroyer *Hayate* broke in two off of Wilkes Island, it was the first sinking of a Japanese warship by an American force in the war. In all, two destroyers were sunk and seven other ships damaged.

Commander Cunningham sent word of the failed invasion back to Hawaii by radio. Standard code procedure at the time required the padding of messages with nonsense phrases. One of the day's dispatches read in part:

SEND US STOP NOW IS THE TIME FOR ALL GOOD MEN TO COME TO THE AID OF THEIR PARTY STOP COMMANDER CUNNINGHAM MORE JAPS…

With the war less than a week old and new reports of American defeats throughout the Pacific coming in almost hourly, the good news from Wake Island assumed the proportions of an instant legend. Someone seized on the words "SEND US" and "MORE JAPS" from the message and soon American newspapers and radios were carrying the story of Wake's "Devil Dog" defenders, who, when asked if they needed anything, replied, "Yes, send us more Japs!" The story reached the men on Wake over shortwave radio.

Yeah, we heard about it. That was the last thing we needed—more Japs.

While the Japanese fleet returned to Kwajalein, the men on Wake endured a daily cycle of bombing and strafing followed by working all night to keep shifting the guns. Fatigue, injuries, and an outbreak of diarrhea took their toll. Casualties kept mounting, supplies dwindled, some of the big guns were damaged beyond repair, and the handful of warplanes fell one by one until December 22 when the last two Wildcats were lost.

On December 15 a relief force of 200 marines and a squadron of Grumman Wildcats sailed from Pearl Harbor. News of the approaching task force reached Wake on December 20 when a Navy PBY landed in the lagoon bringing some hope to the men. Plans were made to evacuate the sick and wounded and all but 350 of the construction workers. The relief force was due to arrive on Christmas Eve, December 24.

On the night of December 22 the Japanese invasion fleet returned with 1,000 amphibious assault troops. The fleet had been built up with the addition of two aircraft carriers, six cruisers and six destroyers to its task force.

It was a moonless, rainy night and the invasion fleet wasn't sighted until 10:00 P.M. At 2:30 in the morning of the twenty-third a landing barge appeared on the beach in front of Battery "F," Lloyd Nelson's position on Wilkes Island. The marines and civilians fought back with machine guns and hand grenades but by 4:00 A.M., the battery was in enemy hands and the gun crew had retreated into the brush.

The gun crew and others on that part of the island regrouped and staged a counterattack on the Japanese who had set up a defensive position in the gun pits. Unknown to them, a second American group had formed on the other side of the battery. The two groups, totaling about fifty marines and civilian combatants, attacked the battery at first light and recaptured the position. By daylight Wilkes Island was back in American hands. The Japanese had lost ninety-eight men. Nine marines and two civilians had died.

Things didn't go so well on Peale and Wake, though. Parts of the islands held out but other parts were overrun. Communications among the scattered forces were cut off, and a message arrived at the island's headquarters informing them that the relief fleet, still 450 miles away, had been recalled. At 7:00 A.M. Commander Cunningham met with Major Devereux and ordered the surrender of the atoll.

Well, we surrendered. Major Devereux and the Japs with a white flag came over and told us to surrender. We could look around the island and that whole damn thing was surrounded by the steel. Boats was circling the island. It's like throwing rocks at a cannon. Our supplies and everything else were getting pretty well depleted, you know, destroyed.

Forty-four American military personnel and eighty-four civilian workers died in the defense of the atoll.

Though Wake's defenders had lost, the victory had been costly for the Japanese. In all, the Japanese lost over 750 men, two destroyers, a submarine and several warplanes. More importantly, the sixteen-day siege of Wake bogged down the Japanese war plan, which called for the early capture of Wake and then Midway for use as an airbase within range of the Hawaiian Islands.

We was captured December twenty-third, marched out to the airport. There was a ditch they marched us past just before you got to the airport and they had put a guy who'd died in there. They'd cut his throat after he'd died and left him there just to show us that they meant business.

We was all crowded in the open, twelve or fourteen hundred of us, all at once, machine guns all around you know. We didn't know what our fate was from minute to minute.

When the war started we took up guns to fight the enemy which is actually classed as guerrilla warfare. And guerrilla warfare against an enemy—that's the firing squad. If you were military you were a little different.

And also, while we were out there fighting it, there was scuttlebutt going around that the Japs don't take prisoners you know. So that puts another chill up your back.

They were held for two days out in the open without food or water. Many of the prisoners had lost their clothing or been stripped of them and suffered from severe sunburn during the day and wet chilly weather at night.

Christmas Day they finally said, "Well, we have orders to take all prisoners to Japan." And then they marched us, so many at a time, to our little barracks. We had to clean those up and had a place to sleep. Then they fed us a little bit.

Between that time and the time we went they had us working out, putting up barbed wire entanglements and stuff like that.

On January 12, 1942, Lloyd Nelson was part of the first shipment of prisoners to leave Wake. The men were brought on board the *Nitta Maru* and forced to run a gauntlet between rows of shouting sailors who struck them with fists and clubs and then were sent down into the ship's holds.

We figured they was going to take us to Japan. They went to Yokohama. We was there, I think, a day or two and they took some guys out to show the Japs that they'd captured some Americans. It was a publicity deal and maybe they were refueling and then they took us from right there down to Shanghai. We got to Shanghai about the twenty-third, about eleven days from Wake Island to Shanghai.

During the voyage from Yokohama to Shanghai,

three American sailors and two marines were blindfolded and brought up on deck. They were beheaded with samurai swords and their bodies were then mutilated and dumped overboard. A postwar war crimes trial determined that their execution was simply an act of revenge for having defended Wake Island.

In Shanghai the prisoners were sent to Woosung Prison Camp. For the next four years the prisoners were fed on scanty rations, about 1,200–1,500 calories per day of low-quality food, and forced to perform extremely strenuous manual labor ten hours a day. Medical supplies and Red Cross packages were often sold on the black market by prison camp supervisors or kept for the camp staff's use.

We had one guy, when we was captured he went to Shanghai, see? He refused to eat the food the Japanese gave you and… Well, he just quit eating and he lasted about a month and he finally just died. He got blind, couldn't hear. He couldn't talk and just faded away. His name was Mark Stanton. I knew him. He worked in the canteen.

Even with the crap they give us, we tried to eat all we could to keep going. One time they had cracked corn and we ate that for two or three days straight. They'd take that and put it in big barrels and let it ferment and then they'd cook it. That's what we ate—just like hog feed.

And then once we had whale blubber and that was so damn rancid that every time you'd belch it'd just burn your throat. It'd stick with you for about three, four days you know. It's a wonder it didn't kill a lot of us guys.

Later on, when I was in Kawasaki, Japan, we tried to dicker with the Japs in their steel mill we was working at. One guy got some fish and he ate it and roll call the next morning they called his name. He didn't answer—he was dead. Died from fish poisoning. His was the top bunk right straight across from me. The covers never moved when they called his name.

After a few months at Woosung they were transferred to Kiang Wang, another prison camp in the area. They were put to work building a rifle range for training Japanese troops and digging a shipping canal. Lloyd's feet froze in the cold winter weather and he suffered from chilblains, a swelling of the hands and feet due to dampness.

We was digging that canal. We'd walk down through the ditch and bring the dirt up and our feet 'd be wet—cold and ice. You never could get warm you know.

Oh, it was cold there, just colder than heck, and that wind coming out of Siberia. You get out in the wind and boy, it'd just cut right through you. Besides, you lost so much weight, you know, there's no fat on your bones to keep you warm.

The prisoners were given particularly brutal treatment at Kiang Wang, with beatings from the Japanese guards. The chief medical officer there, an interpreter named Ishihara, supervised torture sessions.

Ishihara? Yes, he was the uh… He was… He was the damn mean guy—Ishihara.

And then we had a guy we called "Mortimer Snerd." Nicknamed him. He found out what we called him and some of the guys told him, "Well, that's a famous movie actor." And he thought he was pretty proud then. Then later on down the line he figured that's not right and he was madder than hell.

Lloyd contracted beriberi and with his illness and malnutrition, his body weight fell from 195 pounds to 110. In August of 1943 he was sent with a group of prisoners to Kawasaki, Japan, where they worked in steel mills, mines and grain warehouses.

It was "Hurry, hurry, hurry," and shit... you just... You didn't have the energy.

We was loading stuff in a warehouse and I'd just had the flu before that. They was making us stack [sacks like] stair steps, one, two, three—like that you know. Well, I was so damn weak I couldn't do it without falling down with those grain sacks on me.

Them Japs, they'd just kick the shit out of you trying to get you back on it. Then finally, each work party had prisoners there, more or less a boss you know. He told the Japanese, "Hell, that guy's so damn sick," he says, "he can't do it." So then I just loaded the sacks on the guys' shoulders then.

Mel Davidson, of Grants Pass, is another Morrison-Knudsen worker who shipped over to Wake Island at the same time as Nelson. The two men spent the war years together until 1945 when they were sent to different prison camps.

Mel recalls the winter of 1944–45:

That last winter, I didn't think he was gonna make it. He was really in bad shape. It sounds kind of funny, but we used to bet on who was gonna make it through the winter and who wouldn't. He was one of three or four guys that everybody figured was gonna die. I was really surprised when I got back home and found out ol' Lloyd had survived. It's amazing, here it is fifty years later and he's still going strong.

He's a tough one, ol' Lloyd. I mean—not go in a bar and start a fight kind of tough, because that's the last thing he'd do—but he's strong in his body and in his mind. Those old Swedes are a tough bunch. I got to hand it to him: he made it through where a lot of guys didn't.

In all, 117 of Wake's construction workers died in the prison camps. Ninety-eight others who were kept on the island were executed on October 7, 1943. Eight hundred forty-seven made it back to the United States.

American bombers destroyed the steel mills, mining facilities and warehouses in Kawasaki in early 1945. Mel Davidson was sent to Osaka and Lloyd Nelson to Omori Prison Camp in Tokyo Bay.

Lloyd Nelson:

That's where the headquarters for prison camps was. There was a lot of B-29 pilots there you know—just skin and bones. They just starved them to death. A lot of them were litter patients when the war was over. They had to take them out on stretchers.

In Omori I had a fir post next to my bed and that thing was cracked, you know, like when they dry. You looked in there at night and seen all the damn bed bugs, just crowded, like mites in a chicken coop. At night they'd come out and chew away on you. You kill one and that makes the other ones mad and ten more get you. Two nights of that and then the third night you're so exhausted you pass out. They just keep chewing away. Bed bugs, fleas, crabs—anything you could think of they had it.

We was working on the docks there in Tokyo Bay, carrying more weight than we weighed. I got down to 110–115 pounds. The smallest sack of grain was 60 kilos, which is 132 pounds.

There'd be two guys loading onto your back and then you walked across a parking area and up a plank and dump it on a barge. If you didn't get the right spring in your legs, when the plank would come up you'd lose your balance. You had to get the right rhythm.

The barges were hauling supplies inland to safer storage places as American bombers raided Tokyo with increasing frequency. By putting together bits and pieces of information the prisoners could tell that Japan was losing the war rapidly.

On August 14, eight days after the atomic bombing of Hiroshima, the prisoners in Omori Camp were relieved from further work and they waited for the arrival of American forces.

There was not a lot of whoopin' and hollerin'. After four years behind bars, we didn't believe it was over.

The fourteenth of August there was a typhoon, hell of a storm, and they couldn't go in to Tokyo Bay until that was over. So, finally, they come, had their hospital ship and gun boats. It was the twenty-eighth of August that they finally got in to our island and started taking guys off.

They come in there about 2:00, 3:00 in the after-noon. It was just one launch, like a torpedo boat and they said, "Well, we're supposed to take all the stretcher patients first and then go from there on to the healthiest ones the last." I left about 1:00, 2:00 in the morning.

It didn't take them long, maybe about an hour from after they picked us up 'til we was out to the hospital ship and they run us through all the doctors. They's checking for disease, skin troubles and your disposition and stuff like that and asked if you's good enough to go on another boat. He says, "If you don't think you can and you're real bad, then we'll keep you here on the hospital ship. But we have a lot of patients here that if we don't tend to them right quick then they may pass on before they get back home."

Then they sent us down to the galley for our first American meal: ham and eggs and vanilla ice cream with chocolate topping. We sat there just looking at it, we couldn't believe our eyes.

So then they put us on a couple boats and I was out in Tokyo Bay there when the official signing was, all the aircraft above and quite a celebration. I saw all that.

Lloyd was flown from Tokyo to Okinawa and then to Manila where he visited Corregidor before sailing on a new troop transport ship back to San Francisco. After a brief medical exam he boarded a train for Roseburg.

They give us check-ups and stuff and... Just like they say, "Did you report this and report that?" I says, "Hell no. All we wanted to do was get home." Sick or broken back or something, we just... Four years of prison camp, we wanted to get home.

I was telling my wife the other day that I remember when I was coming home on the train. Ashland was a place where trains going south and trains coming north met, and you had about an hour and a half wait there. It was in the afternoon and right close by was a restaurant. So I went up to the restaurant, had something to eat you know.

All of a sudden the siren blew and I thought it was a air raid. I jumped out of my stool and the gal says, "What's the matter?" "That a air raid?" "No, that's the five o'clock whistle." I thought I was still back in air raid range you know. Everything was just on the jittery side all the time.

I got home in October. When I got home a lot of my friends took me out hunting and fishing, trying to get me back into the swing of the American way of life again. I didn't say much about my war experience. I more or less wanted to be by myself. I could only talk to maybe two or three people at a time.

For myself, I can talk about it some and then tonight I probably won't be able to sleep for quite a while but... I've overcome it.

He went back to work for Umpqua Dairy in Roseburg in January of 1946 where he stayed until his retirement in 1973. Physical and emotional problems continued to plague him through the years. Lloyd was hospitalized twice in 1950 for a stress-induced stomach disorder. He suffers from hearing loss, nerve damage to his legs, and back problems.

Despite their combat role and years of internment, Wake's civilian construction workers were not eligible for Veterans Administration benefits until 1981, when an act of Congress granted them military discharges.

Well, that's the government. When we went out there we were civilians working the military bases.

We'd been fighting to get military status because we was fighting right with the Marines. So it's discrimination. There was a lot of work done to it. They finally gave us a discharge and then we didn't have any rating when we checked in for medical problems. "What's your rating?" "N/A—Not Available." So we finally got a full 4-E rating now and that took two, three years to get that.

Lloyd is a member of an ex-POW group, Survivors of Wake, Guam and Cavite. They keep up contact with each other, work to maintain their benefits and hold an annual reunion.

We used to have it every December but due to the weather conditions and everybody's retired, we try to have it in the month of September.

And everybody's getting a little slower—less partying. But then it's a bond between all of us guys that they'll never take it away you know. One guy tries to help another guy if he needs encouragement or something like that.

I just happened to be one of the lucky ones. Just like this picture here: There's Smitty and Hoppy and Bus and myself. This was taken in 1981, we had a reunion then, over in Coos Bay. Smitty died first and Hoppy died next and Bus died next and I'm still here.

This was in a three year time too. They all died from

cancer. Smitty had lung cancer and old Kenny Hopkins had lymphoma and Bus, he had lung cancer and stomach cancer both. And the government don't want to admit it, but I think it's all traced back to malnutrition, forced slave labor and unhealthy living conditions. 'Cause I'd rather sleep out in a sheep shed around Oregon here than back in that prison camp you know.

And you know, all the medical doctors claim that anybody that was in the Japanese prison camps, for every year he spent in prison camp, the inside of his body has aged four years. Like now, I'm seventy-two, the inside of my body is eighty-eight years old.

It seems like somebody just telling you a story. You figure people can't really believe how people can act, how bad they can be. It's not no fiction or anything like that.

Post scriptum: This article was written in 1991. Lloyd O. Nelson passed away December 1, 2011, at ninety-three years of age.

Artless Dodger

When my son was little he lived two lives, one the small, tender and ignorant child whom he was, and the other an imaginary warrior, a hero, tireless, invincible and feared. Little boys shift easily from one existence to the other, live equally in this world and the other, the world of cold fact and the warm imaginary world which underlies it and makes it bearable.

They say that as a fetus we each repeat the evolution of our species, growing from the single cell of Pre-Cambrian seas, to jellyfish, fish, tadpole, lizard, bird, rat, monkey and human and that all these forms lie within us all our lives, buried in layers like an onion. I like to think of that. There is comfort in the notion that what we've inherited lives on inside us, that we are the nine-months' product of a billion years and contain the memory of our long past clear back to the beginning of time.

I like to think sometimes that in our lives from birth onward, having finished those biological steps, we repeat human history in all its stages, from earliest wonder-stricken ape-man to what passes for civilized nowadays, in this age of "guided missiles and misguided men."

He was an amiable barbarian living in the Bronze Age back then, my wily little Odysseus, my half-pint Hercules. Sword in hand, he strutted about the house and yard, defiant and unconquerable. Monsters, demons and even the gods themselves fell before him. Their broken corpses lay in bloody heaps on the living-room carpet and his triumphant shout carried to the farthest edges of the known world. He knew neither compassion nor doubt, only raw will and the strength of his body.

Soft-hearted mothers, their heads filled with liberal notions about raising children, the sort who forbade their children to have war toys, looked on in horror as he slashed his way across the city park playground. The braver ones gently questioned the wisdom of allowing a little boy such imaginary violence.

What could I say?

"Oh, he'll grow out of it," I told them. "He's a little boy—what can you expect?" And once in a while, "Well, you know, I feel foolish asking him not to act childish."

Life, I knew, would eventually surprise him with the knowledge that he himself could die. Only when we doubt our personal immortality do we become compassionate and so, fully human. This, I knew, is the beginning of wisdom, and yet I didn't want to spoil his fun, to take from him his innocence, to rob him of this brazen pleasure. Only once did I try to warn him, to hint at what he would come to understand in his own way.

One day, he stood on the living-room carpet, his battlefield, steely eyed and exhausted amid the carnage of his victims. For a moment he hung by thin threads, caught between the two worlds, unsure whether to launch a new adventure or to rest awhile and eat his soup and crackers like a good little boy. I hope that I spoke from love, but perhaps there was some jealousy too. It's not easy to be a father sometimes, and even grown men often envy the heedless joy of children. I felt the weight of history and he did not.

"You know, son," I told him, "playing the hero is fun, but in real life it's the big, strong heroes who die. You and I, and everyone else, we're descended from men who knew when to run away and hide."

I could see the confusion in his face. I could see that he wondered if maybe he'd done something wrong, that somehow I didn't approve of him. I'd spoken too soon and felt ashamed of myself. I wanted to explain about courage, how it isn't a simple thing, that simply surviving whatever life offers can require more courage than is necessary for a brief bold action. But he, with his uncertain, puzzled look, was too young to hear that.

"It's OK," I said, "Have your fun. Some day you'll understand."

When I was eighteen years old, I made a difficult decision. The bind I was in really had nothing to do with principles, ethics, morality or theology—though I found myself falling back on them as a justification. But no amount of after-the-fact hair-splitting told the truth.

It was something deeper than that: revulsion.

There was a war going on, halfway around the world in Southeast Asia. Faceless old men seated around conference tables in a city on the opposite end of the continent had decreed that tens of thousands of utter strangers in an insignificant corner of the earth must die. The old men were used to killing strangers on command. They'd had their own turn at it and knew full well that strangers don't die willingly; that killing strangers is a dangerous and demanding task requiring young men; that there weren't enough young men at their disposal who would willingly kill strangers.

The old men were crafty and counted on time-tested methods of persuasion which took advantage of our inexperience and insecurity. They spoke noble phrases appealing to our desire to accomplish great deeds. They hinted at the shame and emasculation that cowardice brings. They bluntly stated the consequences of failure to comply with their conscription: ostracism and imprisonment.

It was a systematic process, as formal in its rules and inevitable in its outcome as the stunting and twisting of seedling trees to produce miniature landscapes. The old men, gnarled and dwarfed in their youth by the same process, mistook their decorative house-plant bowls for the world and their own tortured shapes for natural growth. Whatever qualms they may have had lurking in some small unquiet cranny of their constricted souls were sealed in behind an impenetrable wall of numbers, ideology and words.

I and the young men I went to high school with were required to carry a gray paper card proving that we had obeyed the first of these old strangers' strange commands by registering with the Selective Service System. Some of us didn't question what it was that we were being forced to do—not the why of it nor for whom. Others took the first step warily, trusting that it would be possible to avoid both prison and the army by squeezing through one or another of the system's escape holes.

It was a sort of winnowing and sifting of my generation. Of those who registered, some were selected and others were not. Of those who were selected, some served and others did not. Of those who served, some were sent into combat and most were not. Of those who actually battled, some died and most did not.

I chose not to cooperate at all.

It wasn't really a matter of choosing, since the weighing of alternatives and the words of long-dead saints came to me later, after the decision. It was more like instinctively whipping my hand away from a too-hot wood stove, or turning my head at the sight of a gore-drenched car accident. To kill another—the evil was palpable and overwhelming. I could not approach it.

The old men believed that to kill strangers on command was more natural, more fitting, more human than refusing to kill. They believed in competition, trusted in strength, counted on brute force and demanded compliance. They saw evil everywhere but in themselves and in those who carried out their will.

I'd struggled with my own personal anger, which sickened me. I believed in beauty, whose power I felt all around me and experienced daily. I trusted in love, counted on compassion and demanded justice. I saw goodness and mercy everywhere but in my country's leaders.

For six years I lived as an undiscovered criminal, subject to arrest and a five-year imprisonment for not obeying the command of strangers whom I didn't trust or respect. It wasn't an easy time. I struggled with the possibilities, whether or not to confront them openly by forcing them to imprison me, whether or not to seek political asylum in a foreign country, whether or not to stay and make war on my government. I did none of those things, not really knowing why except for a feeling that none of those seemed to fit my situation.

Looking back on it all, I can see that despite the intensely political nature of the times and of my dilemma, I chose to be a criminal out of personal revulsion rather than ideology. I simply couldn't bring myself to either comply with, nor to confront, something so vile that I didn't want any contact with it. I wanted to be left alone, unmolested, unhindered and unattached to anything but what I might happen to meet with through happenstance and recognize as one of God's innumerable aspects.

I made up my mind that, if arrested, I would refuse to cooperate in any way and serve out whatever sentence was given to me. Beyond that, I tried to simply act as though there was no government to support—or to flee from or to struggle against. It bothered me that my choice lacked anything decisive or dramatic. There wasn't anything courageous about it and very little that seemed honorable even to me.

I was young enough to still feel a nearly irresistible temptation toward rebellion and martyrdom, to try to make my life seem meaningful through decisive actions. But I wasn't suited to conflict with evil any more than I was to compliance with it. I hadn't acquired the skills for lovingly opposing what I feared in myself and detested in others.

I lived in a near constant state of internal conflict, doubt and resentment. At times I felt proud, defiant and cynical, at other times humble, subversive and altruistic. In a time of turmoil I'd chosen inaction, a resistance so passive that I'm not sure it could rightly be called resistance.

It's difficult to recall how emotionally charged those times were—difficult, not for lack of memories, but because of how painful those memories are when recalled. The old words—"patriotic," "duty," "democracy," "America"—had lost their meaning. The government's secret bombing of Cambodia and the insurrectionist bombing of America were both carried out in the name of "peace." It was an off-kilter Tilt-a-Whirl world and I wanted, desperately, to walk upright and balanced through it. Each time I staggered I cursed myself and my fellow stumblers and the foreign policy carnies who had lured us all onto their ride. But most of all I resented the ride itself.

Had I known then that my ancestors shared my revulsion towards military service it would have helped me. But I had no helpful past to look to—just a gut feeling that ran counter to what the nation demanded. I didn't know then that there ever had been a legacy of attitudes and feelings, shaped by struggles and desires. I felt but didn't know the source of feeling.

I have friends who speak of past lives, a long cycle of reincarnation. They explain their hidden urges, their inner lives, by saying it is the lives they led before they were born which makes them who they are today. Perhaps it is so, and if so, I am just too dull to know my own former selves.

I could almost accept that comforting belief, but I've noticed that the former lives these friends tell of are always more interesting and more significant than their current ones. People yearn for a story about themselves. We spend our lives looking for explanations, justifications and something which connects us to the past and the future so that the present time is bearable. The tricky part is that all stories contain some truth and none of them contain the whole of truth.

I like to think sometimes that rather than being reborn endlessly in a cycle of past, present and future lives, we are born only once. Yet, in this birth, we are born, not alone, not as an emptiness with only potential, but with the long past of our ancestors, their fears and hopes, their sorrows and joys, their struggles and desires, their failures and accomplishments. Perhaps each of us is the sum of all the long past still reaching toward the future.

Once, I was alone in Strasbourg, where the oldest part of the city lies on an island in the Rhine River. I'd come by train, as a tourist with time to kill and curiosity to satisfy on a little day trip. At least, that's how I explained it to myself later, on the train, after I'd decided to go.

I went, feeling adrift, unsure of who I was or why, worn by weeks of travel in foreign lands, overwhelmed by strange sights and incomprehensible languages and the effort to see and to remember what I saw. I was homesick, tired of my own company, yearning for an end to my sojourn. I went, not knowing what I'd find in the ancient city, vaguely hoping to see some faint trace of my forgotten ancestors, a glimpse into their world.

The island has served as a trading center, administrative capital and fortress since Roman times. It has endured while the empires which seized and lost it came and went. Plague, famine and war washed over it repeatedly. Here, I knew, the world had ended many times and been renewed many times.

I came to a cobbled square near the center of the old city, where a lovely Gothic cathedral, built of rose-colored sandstone blocks, rises. Later, I learned that it is over six hundred years old and took 150 years to build and that it sits on the site of a Roman temple. Despite its massive size and the stubbornness of stone blocks, it does not overwhelm you with unfriendly bulk, but draws you to its warmth and complexity. The intricate details of ornamentation seem natural and perfectly in tune with its towering scale. Like a mountain, the worn building unfolds, playfully revealing itself in the changing sunlight and shadows, in sculpted forms large and small, each part contributing to the whole.

They built lovingly and well, those long-ago people. I was proud of them, proud of their patience, their skill, their sense of proportion, their humble audacity. Some of the builders, at least, were probably Alsatian ancestors of mine, for the further back you trace it, the more ancestors you'll find. It's certain that some of the people whose blood I carry had walked in this square and prayed in this place.

Inside, the cathedral was dark, the walls stained by generations of votive candle smoke, and the feeling of a long continuous human presence was palpable. Some of the tourists seemed oblivious, as though it weren't a church still in use—day trippers dutifully seeing one more sight on a checklist. But most were quiet, aware that they were in a place made holy by unimaginable centuries of human suffering and yearning.

In a little side chapel in the cathedral I found an old wooden pieta, Mother Mary holding the body of her recently crucified Son. I'm not a big fan of Gothic sculpture, with its stiff poses and stylized portraiture, but this one overwhelmed me. The carver had somehow managed to use the restrictive conventions of his time to convey something hauntingly horrible and hauntingly beautiful and utterly human.

The Son was just a scrawny, ugly, broken and mutilated corpse, human in form but without a trace of personality or divinity, only the final impersonal inertness of death.

Her face wore a mother's expression of profound pain, sorrow, regret and compassion.

The two figures told an old story, one more ancient than the event it portrayed, and one that the carver had surely seen played out in his own time—for only direct experience could inform such masterful work. I'd seen the same tableaux myself, in news footage from Bosnia, Chechnya, Afghanistan, Iraq and South Viet Nam. The horror and finality of the corpse, the crushing grief, were the same in old black and white photos from my father's war and in video clips from famine-ravaged Sudan, the debris-strewn streets of Belfast, Oklahoma City and Beijing.

Here, in a side-chapel of a sandstone cathedral on an island in the Rhine, there was nothing I could do except to light a brief candle and pray.

"By the Skin of Our Teeth"

It's hard for most of us to picture the lives of people during the Second World War. The war was so vast and so many people were caught up in it that we often think only of the milestone events and major leaders, forgetting the uncountable personal stories. Like a satellite image of a hurricane, we see its outlines but can't know the reality of being in the storm.

Mrs. V. G. "Kitty" Miller of Roseburg, Oregon, lives surrounded by her memories. The walls, cupboards and bookshelves of her home are crowded with paintings, photos, carvings, and books from the Philippines. For her, a prison camp survivor, the war will always be something very real and personal.

Kitty Miller was eighteen years old in March of 1941, when she returned to her home in Manila after finishing high school in Canada. Born in Manila in 1922, to Canadian citizens Thomas and Katherine Charter, she was named Lucky Kathleen Charter by her father. She grew up in the city, a member of a large community of American, Canadian, British and other nationalities.

I liked it much better before the war. There was peace and quiet and there wasn't too much crime. It was lovely. Everything is in chaos today but it was beautiful before the war. The British had their clubs and the Americans had their clubs. We'd get together and have bowling games and baseball games, dances, celebrations for the holidays and things like that. The club was the only place where you could see most of your friends.

On her return she worked as a secretary in her father's import-export business office in downtown Manila, not knowing that their peaceful, familiar world would be shattered nine months later.

The news of the bombing of Pearl Harbor reached the islands before dawn on the morning of Monday, December 8, 1941, within an hour of the event. By that afternoon Japanese bombers had caught most of the American fighter and bomber planes on the ground at airfields throughout the Philippines, including Nielsen and Nichols Fields in Manila. On December 12, Japanese troops landed in northern and southern Luzon and began their drive toward the capital.

After December eighth it was pretty bad. We'd have to go back and forth to work and the air raids were very numerous. We'd all have to get out of the car and park by the side of the road and look for shelter. And of course, there'd be air raids while we were working. We were on the fourth floor and we were all instructed to go downstairs to the first floor near the elevator, because that was the safest place.

After a few weeks of that we got sort of bored, stand-ing around smoking cigarettes and talking, not being able to finish our work upstairs. Why, father and I ended up just staying in the office and watching the bombing. Most of it was taking place over across the Pasig River and in the port area. We watched them bomb the Incandentia building, which was the mint, right there across the river near Intramuros, the walled city. Like I say, it was pretty hazardous.

More Japanese landings followed on the twen-ty-second and twenty-fourth. While the remains of the American and Filipino armies held out on Corregidor and on the Bataan peninsula, the Japanese army occu-pied Manila on January 2, 1942. Kitty, along with her mother, father, sister, brother-in-law and their two children, left their home in the suburbs and found refuge in Manila.

We were told by the British embassy to get in to Manila because they couldn't guarantee our safety. The location we had to go to was a Catholic school, Assump-tion Convent. We got in there with whatever food we could load up in the car and a suitcase of clothes, an extra pair of shoes and a tooth brush. The nuns were very helpful. They let us sleep on the wooden floor.

Then, about six days later, the Japanese came right into the school [with] open trucks and took us into this big university compound. My father and my boyfriend were already there and they told us to hurry up and get a room because the rooms were filling up fast. So my mother and I ended up on the first floor in a room with twenty-eight other women.

Every third or fourth room would be filled with men. That was on purpose, for our protection. That whole big building was filled up in no time at all with thirty men in one room and thirty women in another, all sleeping on the floor.

We had roll call first thing in the morning and then we'd line up for breakfast. We were only fed twice a day and we'd line up for breakfast, which consisted of either boiled corn or rice and very little else, just a scoop apiece. We had meal cards that had to be punched every time we went through the line to make sure some of the people didn't go in five or six times.

After that, we had to work three hours for the camp. The men would take care of the garbage and the cooking of our meals. The doctors and nurses kept busy all the time. Teachers kept teaching school for the first two years. The third year we were all so weak the kids couldn't concentrate. There was just no way to get them to go to school.

My mother worked in the children's hospital, taking care of the children that got measles and mumps and things like that. My father was a plumber and he converted some of the basins into showers. The only showers were out in the gym where the men were but there was nothing for women and children.

The food would come in through the gate, inspected, of course, by the Japanese. There wouldn't be enough eggs to feed 4,000 people so the eggs that did come in would go to the hospital or the children's kitchen. If a lot of bananas came in we'd each get a banana but if only two or three baskets came in they went to the hospital or the children. For someone like me who was eighteen, why, I didn't see an egg for three years.

There was no bread. There was no flour. The Japanese took everything they wanted first to feed their army and anything left over was what we got.

The only place that we could store anything, clothes, shoes, eating utensils or whatever we had, was under our bed. Private property was under your bed. Everything else was people milling about all over the place. No privacy. No nothing.

We had people that had come down from Shanghai or India and were caught and taken off ships and brought into our camp. It didn't matter what you were, executive or bum—even the whores got caught up and brought into camp—everybody was in there.

You'd constantly hear about somebody's watch was missing or something, and everybody would try to find it. Most of the time they could find it but they were always taking little things.

I had this long hair but I kept it up in braids most of the time—except for when I was washing it. Any time I saw little bits and pieces of soap in the bathrooms, why I'd latch onto them if somebody forgot them. (laughs)

There was always fights out in the hall, two women fighting about some man or something, hair pulling and screeching and the works. There were fights out in the gymnasium where the men were too, about card playing or something. The older men would try to stop the fight before word got out to the Japanese sentries because there would be interrogations and it wouldn't be nice. It was better not to face the Japanese and keep our complaints to ourselves.

As soon as we got in we formed a committee and

any problems that came up we'd take them to the committee. This committee consisted of lawyers and executives—General Electric, Proctor & Gamble, the big companies. If the committee thought that they were serious enough then they'd have to report them to the Japanese.

The only time we took anything to the Japs was when somebody disappeared over the fence or something like that. It happened two or three times. It was pretty devastating.

There were three young English guys who got out in the beginning. They had come in off the ships. They got to the water and hired a banca and were about to take off when they got caught by the Japanese and were made to dig their own graves and (snapping her fingers) were beheaded.

There was some officers who got caught in Cavite out of uniform with their wives, and got picked up as civilians and put into camp. And, by God, if one of the nice, young, tall, good-looking guys didn't snitch and seventeen of them got taken out and put into Cabanatuan, the military camp.

This was a terrible thing to see, this truck coming in and getting these seventeen husbands, who were getting caught out of uniform. It was a terrible thing, to think that there was a snitch in there that would snitch on them. But he got taken too. (laughs) We never saw him again.

During the first year the internees were allowed to purchase extra food from Filipino vendors who came into the camp. The wealthier among them were able to borrow money from Filipino families they'd known before the war. But those who weren't well connected found themselves penniless because all bank accounts had been frozen.

Stan Kidder, a native of Roseburg, Oregon, and his wife Lucia were U.S. government employees stationed in Manila who were also interned in Santo Tomas, where they found themselves in an overcrowded detention camp where food was short and discipline strict.

Stan recalls their efforts to survive:

All sorts of little entrepreneurial schemes were dreamed up to make a little money so you could buy extra food. Some people had nothing and established laundries. Some had enough money so that they could have their clothes washed by hand by internees.

Somebody brought in books. Well, what do you do day after day? Reading's a good thing. So they established a library and you'd go down and take out a book for twenty-five or thirty cents a day.

If you saw a piece of string longer than three inches, you picked it up. If you found an old rust-bent nail, you picked it up and straightened it out. Who knows?—sometime you could use something like that.

Although camp conditions were bad that first year, what followed made it seem relatively luxurious. Stan and Lucia Kidder spoke of the shortages and their effects on the internees. According to Lucia:

We were able to borrow enough money to buy two cases of evaporated milk and a case of canned fish, pilchards—terrible fish, but it tasted marvelous then.

That lasted us for the three years that we were in

there. We would open a can of evaporated milk and it lasted ten days. At the end of the second day or the beginning of the third day, it had maggots in it. But never mind the maggots—you ate it anyway.

The first two and a half years we were able to buy duck eggs. They got increasingly expensive, eight pesos the last time, four dollars apiece, and they were frequently bad. But even the eggs, if you opened them up and set them out in the sun for a while, why, it's surprising how the sun can take the smell out.

I made this pudding with a bad duck egg and sugar with flies in it and cocoa that was actually green—and it tasted marvelous! We gave some to a friend who was really almost starving, just a small amount, about three tablespoons, and he was so pleased. He talked about that twenty years afterward. He was so hungry.

Overcrowding worsened as more civilians were brought to the camp. In the spring of 1943 the Japanese decided to open a new camp at the University of the Philippines Agricultural School located in the village of Los Baños, forty-two miles south of Manila. The town sits between the southern edge of a large freshwater lake, Laguna de Bay, and Mt. Maquiling. Eight hundred men and six Army nurses from Santo Tomas were chosen to build the camp. On May 14, 1943, they boarded a train from Manila to Los Baños. Among them were Kitty Miller's boyfriend, Jay Hinkley, and Stan Kidder.

The men built twenty-two large barracks on the sixty-acre site. The buildings were long, one story sheds with 2x4 frames, thatched roofs of nipa palm fronds and walls covered with *sawili* mats, made of woven split bamboo.

Kitty Miller and Lucia Kidder both arrived at Los Baños in December of 1943 in a group of two hundred women, made up of the wives and girlfriends of men already there. By that time, after nearly two years of captivity, the one thousand internees at the camp were dying at the rate of one person per day.

By the spring of 1944 the camp held 2,200 prisoners including the rest of Kitty's family. The new camp was less crowded than Santo Tomas and for the first time since their capture, married couples were allowed to live together.

Kitty Miller:

I had met my boyfriend in August of '41, before the bombing of Pearl Harbor. I was working and he was working and we would get together on weekends. When the war came along he was a civilian, so he got caught up and thrown into camp too.

When the Japanese finally gave permission for married couples to live together, then young couples asked for permission to get married. By April of '44 we had got married by one of the ministers in camp and before I got out I had a little baby girl.

As the food supply in the Philippines diminished, rations were slowly reduced over the summer and more internees began to suffer from malnutrition and vitamin deficiency-caused diseases.

Lucia Kidder:

In the end there was very little food coming in. The Japanese didn't have it available. They said they didn't have any. We lived not even two miles from coconut plantations. If they would have let some of our men out to go, they would have gotten coconuts and a few things. It was deliberate.

Rats, there weren't many rats, but anything that was edible, earthworms, slugs, we cooked them. If you're hungry enough, you'll eat anything.

The worst thing, probably, was deprivation of food to children. These little children, under ten, needed food to develop their bodies. In almost every case they've had horrible health things. A close friend of ours, who was nine months old when the war broke out, has had to have three hip replacements. Their bones went to pieces. Some had lost all their teeth by the time they were twenty.

In August, Warrant Officer Saadaki Konishi was assigned to the camp and conditions worsened rapidly. Maj. Iwanaka, an elderly officer who commanded the camp, left Konishi in charge of the day-to-day affairs, seldom stirring from his quarters.

When the camp Executive Committee complained of the food shortage, Konishi told them, "You'll be eating mud before I'm through with you." He made good on his threat. The daily ration was reduced from 400 grams of cooked rice in September to 100 grams by December. By Christmas of 1944 the death rate had doubled to two people per day.

Kitty recalls:

The men in our camp, the ones who were dying anywhere from two to five a day, were mostly Spanish-American War veterans, elderly men who were dying of beriberi. You would see the carts come down for burial and they were very, very, very depressing for all of us. To have the desire to live and to see the dead going down the street was very depressing. What can you do?

Two meals a day was so inadequate. Another couple of weeks we all would have had beriberi and all been very ill. There was no way you could live on that forever.

There was hardly any milk left. We got two Red Cross boxes, one from Canada and one from the U.S. and the people who had young children would go around practically begging for the cans of powdered milk that the old bachelors and other people didn't need, just to feed their babies. In the boxes there was cigarettes and candy and stuff like that. Well, they'd trade that for a can of milk for the kids.

Part of the food shortage was due to the disruption of Japanese shipping as the American armed forces worked their way closer to the Philippines. On October 20, 1944, the U.S. Army landed on Leyte. American planes began appearing overhead, passing over the camp on their way to targets on Luzon. The internees were forbidden to look at the planes but the evidence of the Americans' return couldn't be kept from the camp.

On the night of January 7, 1945, the Japanese guards suddenly pulled out of the camp. The internees looted the guard barracks and opened the food warehouse where they found enough rice to double their ration. They ran up the American and British flags and listened to news broadcasts on a short-wave radio set.

The internees stayed in camp, however. It was the

safest place for them, since the Japanese still held their part of Luzon and the southern Laguna de Bay area had many *makapili,* armed anti-American Filipino groups who supported the Japanese.

When the U.S. Sixth Army landed at Lingayen Gulf, north of Manila, on January 9, the internees learned of the landings over the radio and waited anxiously to be liberated.

Five days later, on January 14, the guards returned as suddenly as they had left. Angered by the looting of their quarters, the Japanese again cut their rations, giving the internees only unhulled rice to eat. The rice hulls were hard and sharp and would cause internal bleeding if eaten. The internees spent their days laboriously grinding the rice between pieces of wood in order to get a handful of rice apiece.

With food so short, some of the internees began slipping out of camp at night to beg for food in the village of Los Baños. On the morning of January 28, George Louis, a former mechanic for Pan American Airlines was shot while trying to re-enter the camp.

Stan Kidder:

He was caught coming in—not out. He had heavy bags of vegetables and chickens and whatnot, probably tried to run.

He was pinned down in the hot sun, made to lie out there. Our committee wanted to help him, send him nurses or something. No—shot him. We heard the bullets ring out and we thought, "Oh, thank God, it's over. They're not leaving him out somewhere."

Five days later Kitty Miller gave birth to a

daughter, Karen.

The doctors, while we were in camp, told me that if I ran out of breast milk I was going to have to feed the baby either rice water or coconut milk—whatever I could get. We were so desperate because we had run out of milk months and months earlier. We were having a terrible time. I wouldn't have lasted much longer, feeding the baby.

The U.S. Army closed in on Manila with the 1st Cavalry Division coming from the north and the 11th Airborne Division from the south. Gen. MacArthur ordered the 1st Cavalry to make a dash into Manila. The first troops in Manila, they arrived at Santo Tomas on February 3, freeing 4,000 civilian internees. On February 2, the day Kitty Miller gave birth to her daughter, MacArthur sent a communique to Lt. Gen. Robert Eichelberger, commander of the Eighth Army:

TAKE NECESSARY ACTION TO ASSIGN ONE OF YOUR UNITS MISSION LIBERATING LOS BAÑOS INTERNMENT CAMP PLANNING SHOULD BE STARTED IMMEDIATELY SCAP

The assignment was given to the troops of the 11th Airborne Division (appropriately nicknamed "The Angels"), who were on the southern edge of Manila, some forty miles north of Los Baños.

The 11th was engaged in fierce fighting along the Genko Line, a series of concrete pillboxes connected by tunnels held by thousands of Japanese marines and sailors. They began gathering information on Los Baños immediately, contacting guerilla groups and flying reconnaissance planes over the camp. But the difficulties of dealing with the Japanese at hand and of planning a raid to bring 2,200 prisoners, including children and elderly, many of whom were sick, to Manila from behind enemy lines delayed the start of the raid.

On the night of February 18, three internees, Fred Zervoulakos, Ben Edwards and Prentice "Pete" Miles escaped from the camp. They made contact with Filipino guerillas who smuggled them out of town and across the lake. Pete Miles arrived at 11th Airborne headquarters in Paranaque the next day.

Miles was able to provide detailed information on the layout of the camp, including guard post locations. He also told them what proved to be the single most important piece of information, that every morning from 6:45 until 7:15 all the off-duty guards stripped down to loin cloths and performed calisthenics, keeping their firearms locked up in a shed. The raid was accordingly timed for 7:00 A.M.

Intelligence sources indicated that there were about 250 guards at the camp and another 300–400 troops stationed in the area. Of great concern was the Japanese 8th "Tiger" Division, some 8,000 strong, whose advance units were within a two-hour march of Los Baños.

The plan for the raid consisted of a three-pronged attack. The main thrust would come down a highway along the edge of the lake with trucks to haul out the prisoners. About 100 paratroopers would jump from cargo planes, and, assisted by an advance patrol and 150 Filipino guerillas, would liberate the camp. Three hundred other troops in amtracs would make an amphibious landing from the lake to back them up.

On February 21, Romeo Espino, a leader of President Quezon's Own Guerillas, a local guerilla group, sent a message to Maj. Jay Vanderpool, MacArthur's coordinator for guerilla actions in southern Luzon:

USPIF
HQ., Red Lion Division 25th Div PQOG
In the Field
21 February 1945
URGENT
ESPINO TO VANDERPOOL
HAVE RECEIVED RELIABLE INFORMATION THAT JAPS HAVE LOS BAÑOS SCHEDULED FOR MASSACRE PD SUGGEST THAT ENEMY POSITIONS IN LOS BAÑOS PROPER AS EXPLAINED MILLER BE BOMBED AS SOON AS POSSIBLE PD
W.C. PRICE
COL. GSC GUER
CHIEF OF STAFF

While no documents have ever been discovered which confirm that the internees at Los Baños were indeed scheduled for massacre, in December, 1944, the Japanese Army had issued detailed instructions ordering their troops to kill all allied prisoners rather than allowing them to be liberated.

The scattered army and guerilla units began getting set on the night of the twenty-second for a raid on the morning of February 23. Kitty Miller remembers that morning:

Every morning we had to go out and appear in rows in front of the barracks for roll call. The 7 o'clock whistle blew and we were all half-dressed and ready to run out for roll call and those that got there early saw this plane that went over and had "RESCUE" on the bottom. Well, their eyes bugged out.

That was the signal for the guerillas who had surrounded the camp the night before to open fire on the Japanese guards.

Shortly after the firing started the paratroopers came down. It was the most glorious sight in the world. I mean, 7 o'clock in the morning, to see these paratroopers coming. In concentration for over three years and you think, "Oh wow! We're getting out! We're getting out!"

They landed in the field just outside the camp. They joined in with the guerillas and wiped out the Japanese soldiers, including a bunch who had been doing their calisthenics. They got caught with practically no clothes on.

I guess the skirmish lasted about forty-five minutes. All this time we were laying flat on the floor because of the bullets going straight through the bamboo walls. We were down on the floor covered up with suitcases and mattresses or anything we could get a hold of. I was down there with my little baby.

When the truck convoy was held up by Japanese troops and bridges that were blown up, Maj. Henry A. Burgess ordered the amtrac drivers to evacuate the internees.

We were given twenty minutes to pack a suitcase and get out to the big open grounds that the university used for a parade ground. We packed up quickly and my husband ran out and got all the diapers off the line and we ran down the road. My husband said that there was a dead Japanese on the side of the road. I don't remember seeing him because I was so intent on the baby I guess.

There was a whole line of them, fifty or more all lined up. They could only take so many in each one. I jumped in this amtrac and as fast as they could they started to go down towards the lake.

We drove down to the edge of the water and, by God, if a Japanese machine gun nest didn't open up on us. Those amtracs formed a half-circle right away and aimed their guns at this nest. We're sitting there with the machine guns rattling overhead, all down inside the amtrac and not too long afterwards, why, Navy planes just Zoom, Zoom, Zoom—no more Japanese nest. So then we filed down to the water.

The amtracs were slow-moving vehicles and could only carry about half the internees in the first trip. Lucia Kidder and her husband Stan were in that second group.

Stan Kidder:

We had to walk. It was only about two and a half miles, I guess, but almost everybody had beriberi. There were about 1,000 of us. We walked right through that no-man's land and we had to sit out on the beach waiting for them to come back for us. We finally got off the beach about 5, 5:30 that night.

We got out "by the skin of our teeth," as the saying goes. Not a single person was killed. I was very surprised that we got out.

The second group was also fired on while they waited on the beach and the amtracs crossed over the lake carrying Kitty Miller:

It must have taken about an hour and a half to get to this place, a beach head where the amtracs could get up on the beach and unload us. I was unloaded into an ambulance, because I had the baby. But everybody else was in trucks. And guess where we got?

We were put into the national penitentiary which had been emptied by the U.S. Army and cleaned up. So for the next month and a half we slept on the prison beds.

When we got into the penitentiary the U.S. Army nurses gave us powdered milk, which we made into formula—any kind of milk would have done. That was the field hospital because our troops were still fighting the Japanese and the wounded were still coming into the hospital.

While the battle for Manila raged outside the high concrete walls of Muntinlupa prison, the 2,121 freed internees stayed inside getting adequate medical care and food for the first time in over three years.

Many of the Japanese guards at Los Baños escaped from the raid, including Maj. Iwanaka and W.O. Konishi. Following the withdrawal of American troops from the area, Konishi returned along with Tiger Division troops and *makapili* groups.

Kitty Miller:

When they got in to our camp and found us all gone,

they really took it out on the peasants in the town of Los Baños. There's real terrible stories about what they did to the town people. They accused them all of collaborating and helping the guerillas and the GIs with our rescue. They tied the people up to the stakes on their houses, all these houses were up on stakes. They tied them up and burned the houses down. It must have been horrible.

Maj. Iwanaka is believed to have died of starvation somewhere in southern Luzon before the end of the war. Warrant Officer Konishi was eventually captured and identified. He was tried for war crimes, including the murder of George Louis and the massacre of Filipino civilians at Los Baños. He was executed by the U.S. Army on June 17, 1947.

The battle for Manila continued until March 3, 1945. By then the city lay in ruins. The former internees came out to find piles of rubble where the landmark hotels, offices and government buildings of their pre-war world had stood. Kitty and her family finally returned to their home in the suburbs.

We walked out of our house with suitcases. The only thing left when we got back was the bathtub, and that was sunk in the wall. Everything had been looted, the toilets, the sinks, even the faucets and the pump for the water. There wasn't anything left.

What the Japanese didn't take, the Filipinos took. They needed money. They'd take it down to Chinatown and borrow some money on it to feed their kids.

My father refused to leave because his business and his home and everything was in the Philippines. So he stayed behind and mother and sister and brother-in-law, their two kids and myself got on a ship, the Eberle, *and we were repatriated to the States.*

When dad stayed he had a heck of a time. Manila was so badly demolished that there wasn't any place worth staying in. So he stayed with an ex-employee of his and had to beg rides every morning from the army. The streets were so badly bombed that there was clouds of dust for miles and miles where the army trucks and jeeps were whizzing by.

Kitty and her husband lived for a while in the United States but the post-war recession brought them back to Manila in 1947. Her husband suffered from severe depression and was later found to have schizophrenia. He returned to America leaving Kitty and her three daughters in the Philippines. She never saw him again.

She met V.G. Miller, an army combat photographer who had come to Manila following his discharge and was working as a stringer for United Press.

When Jay left for the States his friend was opening up this photo studio in Manila and I was terribly interested in photography anyway. So, when he needed somebody to work in his studio I went to work for him. I ended up working in the studio for twenty-seven years with my new husband. Later on we had two children of our own.

Stan and Lucia Kidder also remained in the Far East. Stan went to work for the State Department following the war and served in many posts throughout Asia until his retirement in 1962. That year the Kidders returned to Roseburg where they live in the house where Stan was born.

The Millers moved to Roseburg in 1976 when the political situation in the Philippines became dangerous under the Marcos regime. They finished raising their children there and lived together until Kitty's husband's death in 1990.

Post scriptum: Kitty Miller passed away on December 26, 2012, at eighty-nine years of age. Mr. and Mrs. Kidder have also since passed on.

Of Flower Power
and the War With the Newts

*Written in 1996, this commentary is an historical
artifact now, which, come to think of it,
is pretty much what I've become.*
—R.L.H.

The Speaker of the House has said that he wants
to undo the effects of the 1960s hip counterculture on
American civilization and no one he's talked to lately
knows enough about the era to laugh in his face. Believe
me, the stone-cold hippies of old would have found the
notion hysterical—yet more proof that the cosmos
really does have a sense of humor. Apparently, Newt
Gingrich and a lot of other "Mr. Jones" types just weren't
in on the joke.

I guess you'd have to have been there.

To appreciate the absurdity of the situation, you
need to understand that most of what passes for sober
analysis of the sixties is based on things acid freaks told
credulous reporters as a practical joke. If you were hip,
you knew it was all jive; if you weren't hip you got jived.

By and large, the American public wasn't hip—
they ate it up, in the form of lurid magazine and newspaper articles and in gaudy "psychedelic" wares
peddled by head shop hucksters. People were eager to
grasp at anything that seemed to make sense of what

was happening and "sex, drugs and rock 'n roll" not only appealed to nearly everyone's secret fantasies but sold a lot of tacky merchandise as well. Besides, the truth wasn't believable or marketable to editors or to the public.

It was all great sly fun at the time. The wilder the stories got, the happier everyone was. Reporters got spicy copy; the public got titillation; hippies got a good laugh; hip and not-so-hip entrepreneurs made piles of money. A few uptight people were outraged over what they heard was going on but never actually experienced, but for the most part it was all very innocent and juvenile—as innocent and juvenile as the hippies themselves were.

The Flower Children were, despite the official line at the time and since, highly moral people. Improbable as it seems, walking around buck naked on some backwoods commune was not a terribly prurient activity—the average beach-party beer commercial of today comes closer to pornography. Shedding your clothes was just a way of shedding the tawdry odor of stag-film-night cigar smoke by saying "You're not Barbie and I'm not Ken so let's stop pretending that we are."

Of course, most people didn't grasp the difference between casting off bogus stereotypes and licentiousness. To be hip meant, in part, to know the difference, and those who didn't know were more to be pitied than scorned. What Newt, Rush Limbaugh, Cal Thomas and other proponents of an anti-sixties counter-revolution have declared war on is a myth they bought into—of an explosion of immorality—because they never understood what was actually happening.

What really happened was both more startling and more prosaic than anyone could have imagined. It was a private spiritual event, an epiphany that took place over and over again, at different times and in different situations for everyone who went through it. This simple change of perception had profound moral, political and social implications, but, despite its overwhelming nature, it was inexpressible, except through laughter.

What confused things was the attempt, sometimes quite earnestly and sometimes as the grossest put-on, to explain the inexplicable. "Are you experienced? Have you ever been experienced?" asked Jimi. Those who were couldn't hide it. Those who weren't couldn't fake it well enough to fool those who were, though they often fooled themselves and others who weren't.

There were, in the decade or more leading up to the Summer of Love, an enormous number of lonely people—nerds, fairies, dykes, poets, fat people, poor people and other losers—who just didn't fit into the rigid roles that our society officially approved of. It was a time when appearances—of success, of normalcy, of morality and patriotism—were more important than realities. They, the lonely, believed deeply in the illusion of who a modern American was supposed to be and blamed themselves for failing to meet that impossible standard. The sense of shame kept them isolated from each other.

There are many theories as to why the American Dream suddenly lost its hold, but the fact remains that an inevitable miracle occurred repeatedly—all across the land, the children saw that the emperor had no clothes and laughed at the trappings of authority. The resulting outburst of laughter left pundits scratching their heads and "Better Dead than Red" politicians scurrying for subpoenas, looking for an explanation for the sudden appearance of all these giggling weirdoes. But the joke was on them and they never did figure it out. Groucho Marx was closer to being the counterculture movement's philosophical grandfather than Karl.

It was the revolt of the misfits. One by one these lonely outcasts realized that it was the world itself that was weird, not themselves. The spontaneous outburst of individual laughter at this discovery led to a second, even more joyous discovery: they were not alone. There were other misfits out there, perhaps millions, who'd seen the utter absurdity of trying to live as round pegs in a world of square holes. A shared compassion and delight brought them to love each other. Then it was too late: the change had already come and they were no longer afraid. Everything since has been side effects.

Of course, there were many who never let go of their fear and rejected the chance to trust the power of love. Now, almost thirty years later, you still find nearly every member of my generation living out the effects of those years. Those who were truly hip remain so, quietly following the lessons which came out of moments of bliss; those who never were hip are still bitterly denouncing the joke they never caught on to.

Perhaps the greatest irony of this anti-sixties jihad is its irrelevance. "Stuck in the sixties" has been a pejorative phrase for quite a while in conservative circles, a way to dismiss those years as a very sour bunch of grapes. Yet those who deride and those who defend the counterculture of thirty years ago are equally stuck in the past. By engaging in the debate, my generation has finally become useless old fossils whose opinions don't matter.

It's the nineties, folks. There's a whole new smirking generation out there who see quite clearly that we're morally and intellectually bankrupt. I wish for them, one and all, peace and much love.

Grapes of Joy

Until now, you never knew another home. All your life you've spent here in our little valley, where winter snows sit on the ridge tops like white trim on a fragile green bowl, a small world amid the sleeping mountains, circular like an island in the sea. To you it seemed inevitable, not one of many possible worlds but the world itself, and every place else seems different because it is not this.

Yet we chose this place, your mother and I, from among the uncountable possibilities the earth offers. We chose it not just as a place where we, two lovers who are friends, would live, but where we two would become three.

I remember a friend joking that we were "doing the Okie thing—only backwards," leaving California in an old battered pickup truck and heading to the countryside. Like tens of thousands of others at the time, we wanted something different than the chance to make money. It was an escape from the spiritually impoverished world of urban America rather than the hard economic necessity of poverty, foreclosure and hunger which had brought our parents' generation from the boondocks to the city.

Southern California was no longer the sunny orange-scented paradise of the late 1930s. We looked around us and saw smog, traffic, the alienating asphalt landscape, crowding, a place beset by twin plagues of criminals and police. Working out of doors most of the time, I became alarmed at just how much of the landscape had become inhospitable to people, used up by streets, freeways, parking lots, or fenced off with chain-link fencing and razor-edged concertina wire. It wasn't a good place to own a dog, and the prospect of raising a child in such a place seemed like cruelty. Our lives, if we stayed, seemed destined to become as stark and artificial as the world we lived in. We yearned for something smaller in scale, something more real and direct, less confined.

Our lives had become more comfortable and this, in itself, seemed like a threat. After a few hardscrabble years of unlicensed "contracting," the house painting jobs I acquired were beginning to pay better. I no longer needed to advertise. Word-of-mouth was bringing me wealthy clients in Beverly Glen, Laurel Canyon, and the "Swish Alps" above Hollywood, instead of cheap, hurried work on run-down homes in Northeast L.A. on the edge of the Barrio. Yet the lives of these wealthy people seemed somehow emptier, less fulfilling, than the life I wanted. I worried about getting fat and lazy and squandering my life in the pursuit of "someday."

Everywhere, it seemed, we met people who had the same goal—to leave. "Screw L.A., we're getting out of here," they'd tell us and we'd nod our agreement. The city's days seemed numbered. People speculated openly about how much longer it could possibly last before it either vaporized in a big white nuclear flash or collapsed, if not courtesy of the San Andreas Fault into the Pacific, then under its own suffocating dystopian weight. Apocalypse now or later: either way, we, and thousands of others, didn't want to be there when it happened.

It was a heady time, a movement was underway, an adventure, and we were part of it. Beyond the desire to escape was the feeling that somehow we were changing not only our own lives but also turning our society's life around. Five years earlier we'd believed in an imminent brief violent upheaval that would usher in a radically new way of doing things. Now we saw ourselves as part of a quieter, more personal revolution, equally idealistic but more profound.

My oldest brother, your Uncle Jim, had moved to southern Oregon four years before, and we'd seen the lovely green mountain country on visits, heard that the wages were decent and the land prices were reasonably cheap.

We left in Bertram, a 1948 Chevrolet Thriftmaster three-quarter-ton pickup, heading north on Interstate 5 with our possessions piled in the back and my uncle Joe's twenty-year-old homemade camping trailer hitched behind. Five years before we'd lived for weeks on end out of a single backpack, hitchhiking to distant places at will. Now we carried a half ton of more-or-less worldly goods—furniture, tools, books, stereo and records, clothes—piled high between the truck's wooden side racks.

The old beater rocked and swayed along Interstate 5,

up over the Grapevine and through the Great Central Valley where the dust bowl migrants' dreams had withered forty years before. Unperturbed by the weight of history, the burden of possessions and the curses and up-thrust fingers of hurried travelers, Lonesome Pickup Bert kept a steady pace of fifty miles per hour uphill and down and across the flats.

The journey took two long days. They were delicious days, a feast of self-congratulatory relief and naive anticipation spiced by uncertainty.

We'd intended to find a small farm near my brother's place in Days Creek, but there were too many new settlers arriving with the same dream and not enough rural acreage to house us all. Land prices were rising fast and "Californian" had become a local pejorative term. After three weeks we found a small rental, part of an old pink triplex on a city street in Myrtle Creek.

It was our eighth change of address in five years. This time, we planned to stay—in the area at least, though not in the triplex. More than anything we wanted permanence, a place we could love, a place we wouldn't have to leave. We hadn't words for it then, just an overwhelming sense of freedom, joyful to be freed from so many things we'd yearned to escape, grateful for what our new stomping grounds were not.

It was, in many ways, a time of infatuation, like it is when two lovers find each other and their shared joy in the end of loneliness is enough for their beginning. Later, the work comes and with it, if the work is care-filled, the necessary understanding and compassion. Freedom from things can seem silly then, when you've found freedom within what you have made.

The Watchers

*D*riving upriver, a dark round shape emerges from the brush and crosses the road ahead. You slow down and peer through the windshield as two smaller ones follow. The swift undulating forms suddenly make sense, a black bear and her two cubs disappearing into the roadside greenery just as you realize what they are. And now they're gone and the forest depths hide their secrets again.

You remember again what you had forgotten, and then you grin. Two worlds live side-by-side, though seldom touching, and so you doubted the evidence of your own eyes at first. The human world of glass and steel, of paychecks and politics had seemed all the world there was until the sudden appearance of these dark unexpected beasts reminded you that the ancient order somehow lives on too.

It's still there, the old-time world, and just as mysterious as ever. You pass through it every day, hurrying along in your headlong rush while just a few feet away mystery lies hidden in the brush.

How many eyes have watched you go by? Cougar,

bear, elk and bobcat, quiet and wary, frozen for a moment and then moving off again once you're gone. How many times has Old Man Coyote, the trickster of Northwest myths, laughed at you and at the whole two-legged race while standing behind a tree or lying low while sunning himself atop a rock face?

Who really knows what goes on in the world hidden within our little world? If we can be surprised by something we knew was possible, even likely, then what other things are we missing? Unlock the doors of perception and there's no telling what might walk in on us. If we could slow down enough, could we hear a rock singing? If our ears were attuned, could we listen in on the whispered gossip of trees?

We walk through this place like characters in a playhouse farce passing through the same room moments apart and never guessing that the other is there.

The Improbable Adventures of Hathaway Jones

In 1903 Claude Riddle, along with his brother Ernest and A.R. Mattoon, went prospecting in the mountains along the Rogue–Umpqua divide up the West Fork of Cow Creek.

For a month they camped in the hills and searched the steep canyons but came back empty-handed, a typical prospecting venture in those days when many searched the hills for wealth but few ever found it. The trip was so commonplace that it was hardly worth noting if not for a literary gold mine in the unlikely form of a local muleskinner named Hathaway Jones.

Fifty years later Claude Riddle wrote about the man whose fabrications earned him a listing in the library catalogues as an author although he never wrote a book or story.

After we had been there for a week or two and my brother had taken some samples home for assay and had no satisfactory result, we decided to move. We had lost touch with the outfit that packed us in, so Mattoon had gone to Mule Creek and spent the night. On his return next morning he said, "Hathaway will be in here soon to pack us over to Gold Mountain." We had decided to spend a few days there before returning home.

We were busy assembling our outfit, when we heard the jangle of bells and the scuffle of horse's feet on the trail. Some unintelligible human calls were heard from the approaching cavalcade. It was Hathaway directing his animals. The file of horses and mules meandered down from the trail to the flat where we were camped and Hathaway appeared in person.

He was small and short and walked with a forward stoop. His arms were long and his hands seemed to swing ahead below his knees. Later I saw him in profile walking up a hill, taking such long steps that his body bobbed up and down, giving the impression that he was walking on four legs. He wore a conical little black hat with a buckskin string woven in for a hatband. His heavy blue flannel shirt was open and black hair decorated his throat and breast. A narrow leather belt held his pants about his slim hips and it looked like he might come apart in the middle any time. Hathaway's speech was most peculiar—a cross between a hair-lip and tongue-tie. His pronunciation of some words was intriguing, and he always seemed in dead earnest.

While we were getting the packs on, Hathaway told me about his "animals." "Now this little bay mule, Dandy," he said, "he's one of the best I've got. He can carry a pack just as careful, never bumps trees or anything, but he gets stubborn streaks when I can hardly do anything with him. He just won't do nothin'. Stubbornest thing I ever saw. He's stubborn as a damn mule."

Riddle was amused by Hathaway's appearance,

odd speech and off-hand manner of joking with a straight face. Later he learned, to his delight, that he was listening to southern Oregon's greatest liar.

"So, you didn't find your ledge," Hathaway remarked. *"A year or so ago I was drilling some holes on the face of a ledge over on Cattle Creek, and I heard the bells on the 'animals' startin' out the trail for home. I dropped everything and ran to head them off, and didn't get back to the ledge for a month or more. When I did come back the gold was just oozin' out of the drill holes."*

During the days that followed, Riddle heard a dozen or so tall tales from the imaginative muleskinner—stories which impressed him enough that fifty years later he still recalled them and the way they were told. In a land full of unusual characters, Hathaway Jones stood out.

Our past here in southern Oregon is difficult to sort out at times. The colorful people and events of the early years sometimes seem exaggerated even when truthfully told. In the case of Hathaway it becomes even harder to separate fact from myth because the facts are few and exaggeration was the stuff of his life.

Hathaway Jones was born in Roseburg on October 28, 1870, the third of eight children. His father, William Sampson "Sam" Jones, came to Oregon in 1853 as a twelve-year-old boy with his family. Hathaway's grandfather, Isaac "Ike" Jones, took up a donation land claim near Roseburg and built Roseburg Flouring Mills along Deer Creek. Sampson married Elizabeth Luserbia

Epperson in 1863 and they were divorced in 1883. Sampson, who seems to have been something of a ne'er-do-well, worked as a bartender in Roseburg. In 1890 he and Hathaway moved to the Rogue River country, eventually settling at Mule Creek.

As we set about to prepare our dinner, I peeled some potatoes. Hathaway said: "You'd ought to seen the spuds we had over on Mule Creek. I planted some in new ground above the cabin, One day I says to pa, 'I'm goin' up and see if them taters are big enough to eat.' So I goes up and digs into a hill; about two bushels rolled out before I could stop up the hole."

Hathaway became a mail carrier in 1898, packing the mail by mule train, from Dothan, a whistle stop at the West Fork of Cow Creek, to Illahe on the lower Rogue. For most of those years he was employed by Charles Pettinger of Illahe. He married Flora Thomas sometime early in the century and they lived for a while on Mule Creek near Marial, raising a son and daughter. Like his father's marriage, Hathaway's ended in divorce. Following the divorce, he boarded with Charles and Sadie Pettinger at their Big Bend Ranch where he stayed until his death in 1937.

Born with a cleft palate and harelip, Hathaway's speech defect could have left him cut off from his neighbors, marked as a freak. Instead, he managed to use his handicap as an asset for gaining acceptance, popularity and eventually, local fame.

He was a funny-looking man, with a thick black

mustache (grown to hide his harelip) set beneath a large nose, and he had a funny way of talking. His appearance and speech kept him from being taken seriously but added to his exaggerated stories and dry one-liners.

Though folklorists classify his yarns as tall tales, Hathaway was simply considered to be a liar, a title he took a great deal of pride in, allegedly once threatening *The Oregonian* with a libel suit when that paper named someone else as the state's biggest liar.

On the trail one of the packs got a little askew and we stopped to right it. I rolled rocks down the hill to see them splash in the creek a hundred yards below the trail. "Over on Bear mountain," said Hathaway, "I was hunting one time, and on the brink of a little steep canyon I saw a rock, round as a ball and 'bout two feet through, just sittin' there waitin' for some one to push it off. I shoved her off and down the hill she went and up the other side just about level with me. Back she come, right up to me again; down she'd go and back she'd come. I watched till I got tired of it and went on. About six weeks afterward I went back that way and I see a deep ditch worn down on each side of the canyon and stood there lookin' when I heard a little rattle and here comes that rock up to me. She was worn down to about the size of a marble."

In those days, before phonographs, radio and television, the arts of conversation and oratory were highly developed. Debates between local small town figures were popular, and people would travel long distances to hear a popular speaker such as William Jennings Bryan.

The public speakers of the day studied literature,

rhetoric, and elocution and borrowed techniques from the theatre, often unconsciously falling into the iambic pentameter of Shakespearean drama in their delivery. It's hard to imagine such patience in this era of the ten-second sound bite, but, as a reading of any of the Lincoln-Douglas debates will show, a gifted orator could hold an audience's attention for hours.

Jones' stories came out of an ancient tradition of telling exaggerated stories. Boasting was a well-established custom among Europe's Celtic, Germanic and Scandinavian peoples. Mike Fink's famous boast is a good example of early nineteenth century American lying.

A good liar was an important man in those days and every community had someone who could be relied upon for a well-told whopper. Hathaway wasn't the only liar in southern Oregon, but he was the best.

"I was huntin' one day and I see this two-year-old bear off about 362 yards and a quarter sittin' up on his haunches eatin' a mushroom about as big as a half-dollar. I shot and he begun turnin' over and over down through the salal brush, makin' more noise than drivin' a four-horse team through the woods draggin' a dry bullhide. When I go over where he was he was layin' there moanin' and dying, but the first thing I knew he got up and come at me just like like a bitin' sow. I got him killed and took him home. Fat, you never saw the like. I guess he would weigh 200 pounds. I rendered him out and got about 375 pounds of bear grease out of him."

Most of the old time liars are unknown and their tales are fragmentary. But Hathaway's have been passed along, not just in outline but much as he told them. They make up one of the largest collections of tall tales from a single known teller in American folklore. Fifty-eight of them were collected in 1974 and published as *Tall Tales from Rogue River, the Yarns of Hathaway Jones,* edited by Stephen Dow Beckham, by the University of Indiana Press and re-issued in 1991 by Oregon State University Press.

The stories feature not only Hathaway but also the adventures of his grandfather "Ike" Jones as a wise old mountain hermit who could speak the language of the animals and of his father, "Sampson" Jones, who was nursed by Ike's pet cougar when his mother died in childbirth.

The all-too-real everyday dangers of living in remote country—rattlesnakes, bears, cougar, avalanches and game wardens—were exaggerated in Jones's stories. But Hathaway and his kin always managed to overcome them with an unexpected feat of strength or cunning. And when the tale revolved around a commonplace achievement—catching salmon, raising melons or potatoes, building a fireplace—they simply did it far better than anyone else.

You'd ought to have some of the draft we had in the fireplace pa and me built in our cabin. We carried up a pile of big rocks and then mixed ashes and clay for mortar and put about a sack of salt in it. After we got the fireplace built we got a joint of big mine pipe for the chimney and I found a short piece of pipe that was littler at one end and put it on top like a nozzle. Pa says, "We'll let her dry out plenty 'fore we build any fire."

After we got the punchin floor down, we started squarin' the walls with an adz. The floor was all piled with chips, and pa says "I'm goin' to scoop some of this stuff into the fireplace and burn it so maybe we can find the floor."

The chips and shavings begun to burn right now, and she commenced to get hot. Perty soon she begins to suck and roar, and she started draggin' the chips off the floor and into the blaze. Pa and me run outside, and she sucked that cabin as clean as if we'd swept it.

Despite the boastful character of his tales, Hathaway himself is said to have been a modest, easy-going man. The yarns seem to have been made up simply to amuse his listeners and fill them with a sense of wonder. Although he was known to be fond of "white rye" moonshine whiskey and his conversation "wasn't fit for parlor talk," none of his contemporaries reported any lewd talk, rowdiness or spitefulness on his part.

When Alice Woolridge interviewed Charles and Sadie Pettinger in 1967, she found them reluctant to talk about him: "They wouldn't talk: said he was a nice old man and all the funny remarks he made were about himself or something that happened to him. They were afraid that people would ridicule him and they said he never said anything about other people."

In September, 1937, Hathaway's mule appeared at Marial without him and a search party was organized. Following the trail back toward Dothan, they found his body at the foot of a cliff along the trail, apparently thrown by his mount. Ironically, one of his tall tales told of how he'd survived just such a fall when his mule, startled by a rattlesnake, jumped off a cliff and Hathaway had the presence of mind to pull back on the reins in mid-air and holler "Whoa!" bringing his mount to a stop just before they were both dashed on the rocks below.

Fortunately, his stories survived him. They have been retold over the years by those who heard them from Hathaway and their descendants. Arthur Dorn, a writer who lived in Agness in the late 1930s and early 1940s, collected several tales both from Hathaway himself and from local people who'd heard them. Dorn's versions are longer, more complex and considerably more polished than Hathaway's homespun style and speech defect allowed, but they contain elements that would have been lost otherwise. Other writers from time to time have produced more or less accurate retellings of Hathaway's yarns for magazines and newspapers over the years.

Sorting out the stories attributed to Hathaway is difficult. He seems to have re-worked the tales over the years, producing many variant versions. He also picked up older stories and shaped them to his own peculiar style, and it's likely that since his death, some tales he never told have been attributed to him. But which ones are genuine, which are original, and which are apocryphal is often not clear.

He was buried near Marial in a small graveyard overlooking Battle Bar on the Rogue River. By the time of his death his fame had spread statewide and *The Oregonian* took note of his passing in an editorial:

The story which tells of the passing of Hathaway Jones presents him as being distinctly a character, with a shrewd and merry wit. Now here is a problem: do the far silent places shape such men, or do such men seek out the remote canyons to build their cabins back of beyond? Lord, how we envy them sometimes, these fellows like Hathaway Jones, who seem to have soaked up the very flavor of the firs or the prairies. The sea has that way with some men too. It is evident that living in towns and belonging to literary societies, or luncheon clubs and lodges, somehow doesn't do half so much for us as the Rogue River canyon does for such men as Hathaway Jones. Somehow they seem to have been going to school all the time, by themselves, at some sort of college. And maybe they have.

Dialoguing With Eric

$\mathcal{W}$e were working a Cat show upriver. I was setting chokers behind a D-6 and doing a little bucking between turns. It was still lacking an hour until noon when the boss gave me the "load up" sign. I climbed up on the Cat and shouted, "What's up?"

"Come on in," Larry yelled back. "Damnedest thing I ever seen."

We couldn't talk much above the diesel roar, and old Larry's a little on the deaf side anyway, so I just hung on while we clattered in to the landing with our logs. I figured that we'd had another breakdown. Larry's equipment wasn't exactly what you'd call new, but he could fix most anything if you gave him a pair of pliers, some wire and a welding torch.

The first thing I saw when we got to the landing was a little car all plastered with bumper stickers, parked next to the water truck like a calf grazing next to a cow, and a young dude sitting politely on the hood.

"Who's that?" I shouted.

Larry shrugged, "Don't know," and jerked his thumb over his shoulder, a sign for me to jump down and chase for him. Setting and chasing chokers behind a Cat you have to use sign language a lot—logger signs, not the quick little finger movements of deaf folks, but great big obvious stuff, waving arms and clenched fists or a hand pointed straight up to the sky. Standing next to a bulldozer that's ready to lurch into action, a man doesn't want his directions to the Cat skinner misunderstood. So we waltzed through the paces: "slack line," "jump in," "pop the bells loose," "jump out," "roll 'em up," "stop," until I hung the choker cables up on the back of the Cat.

I got back out of Larry's way, and he did a neat spin, backed up, lowered the blade and pushed the logs to the top of the log deck. Larry skins Cat with a grace that's a joy to see, with never a wasted motion or a moment's hesitation. I looked over to see if the guy on the car was suitably impressed. I figured he must be looking for work—lot of folks out of work these days. But he didn't look like a logger or a tree planter, more like a college kid actually.

Larry backed down off of the log deck, throttled down and waved me over to the Cat. "I can't understand a word he's saying," said Larry, pointing at the fellow. "Go see if you can figure out what he wants."

Poor ol' Larry, too many years of running a chainsaw without ear plugs, probably embarrassed to make the guy speak up. He was a young guy, about my age maybe, but everything about him seemed younger somehow, shiny-bright like a new penny and a little self-conscious.

"What's happening man?"

"Hi!" he says and holds out his hand. "I'm Eric,

from the Northwest Biocentrism Institute, a non-profit educational organization promoting the conservation of natural resources and the development of community-based sustained resource economies."

"I'm Bill Soffer, from Riddle," I told him and shook his hand.

"I'm doing community outreach, and I'd like to speak to you and your employer about some of the socio-political and economic issues which are impacting this region."

"Oh… You from Eugene?"

"No, Portland."

"Oh. Well… OK. Let me go talk to the boss."

Well no wonder Larry came and fetched me in. "He's a hell-raiser," I told the boss when I got back to the 'dozer. "Wants to talk to you and me."

Larry looked over at the stranger, checked his pocket watch and looked at the log deck. "Hell's bells," he said, "I thought he was a salesman." Larry likes hell-raisers. His grandpa was in the I.W.W., and Larry himself has a scar on the back of his head some company men gave him during the timber faller's strike twenty years ago. "Well, let's eat dinner early, and see what he's got to say. Maybe you can interpret for me."

So that's how I ended up sitting on a log between Larry and this Eric character so that they could talk to each other. Eric would say something and then I'd put it into the boss' language, and then Larry'd say something and I'd do the same thing the other way. I've never been to college, but I've read a stack of books like you wouldn't believe; so it wasn't hard really. Eric reminded me of a tree planting foreman I had for a couple months one winter, a guy with a master's degree in forestry who couldn't tell a porcupine pill from an elk dud. Anyway, interpreting was kind of fun, though it was hard to take time out for a bite of sandwich now and then.

"We at the institute feel that the pervasive depletionary paradigm is too narrow of an approach to regional sustainability issues. The profit motive which actuates the multinational corporate structures that dominate our resource base causes a growing dichotomy between the well-being of our bioregion's inhabitants and the requirements of capital-intensive industry."

"He says he don't like the way things are run around here. The big outfits are too money-hungry, and they're putting the squeeze to the little guys."

"Ain't that the truth," says Larry. "But what're you going to do about it?"

"Larry says he recognizes the validity of your assumption regarding the economic basis of the negative impacts of large corporate structures on rural communities and wishes to know what type of social re-vitalization programs you visualize as being relevant to this situation."

"Are you from Eugene?"

"No, Riddle."

"Where's that?"

"Downriver."

So we had a good time, the three of us, and Eric especially was real happy to be dialoguing with ol' Larry. Larry invited him to come watch us drop a tree, but Eric wasn't into it. Eric asked me if I was interested in doing some community outreach like him but I wasn't into it.

I like to do things more than I like to talk about doing things.

"You really should be doing community organizing," Eric told me. "With your ability to empathize with non-countercultural persons you could provide your community with a valuable interface for raising consciousness on social change issues."

"No, that's OK. Larry's a good guy to work for."

Well, we'd emptied our nose bags and had a nice chat, and Larry didn't see any logs coming in on their own, so it was time to get back to work. Eric shook our hands and drove off just as happy as could be and me and Larry walked back to the Cat.

"Well, what do you think Larry? You gonna jump on the bandwagon with him?"

"Him?" says Larry. "Oh, he's OK. Still just a pup —we'll see whether he's worth anything in a fight after he loses his milk teeth."

Where Angels Fear

$\mathcal{I}$t was late morning on a hundred-dollar day when I slipped. Most on-the-job accidents are caused by carelessness, and if this one had been I wouldn't still be wondering about it today, over twenty years later. But it wasn't an oversight or clumsiness that left me inexorably sliding toward the edge and trying to do the right things after I'd made the wrong choice.

My younger brother and I were shingling a roof that day, back in 1974. Actually, since we were just beginning the job, he was shingling, setting the first courses and toe irons from his perch atop an extension ladder. I was at the opposite end of the steeply pitched gable, about twenty feet up in an avocado tree with a saw in hand, trimming branches away from the eave.

It was a large old two-story house with a rotting roof that, according to the tenants, had been leaking for at least five years. I was enjoying the work, up there in the shade on a sunny morning, feeling the curved branch beneath my crepe-soled shoes, dropping the severed limbs down to the lawn below as I trimmed them off.

I was feeling even more cat-like than usual, a feeling that is one of the secret joys of a steeplejack. To move with assured grace, to climb and balance unafraid up above the earth-bound world of ordinary people with their mundane concerns is to feel an exhilarating kinship with the angels. You watch from above as the small figures pass by below, men and women who almost never look up to see you balanced there between heaven and earth.

The feeling was strong in me that morning and with the sunlit slope of the faded red shingles rising before me, just inches away, it occurred to me that I could easily step out of the tree and onto the roof.

Believe it or not, it seemed like a good thing to do at the time. I was used to plying a dangerous trade, was quite good at it in fact, and the green roll of fifty-dollar bills the contractor handed me every week was proof of that. I accepted the risks as I accepted the cash, gladly and with a sense of pride.

I stood on the branch and studied my route. About fifteen feet up the roof and fifteen feet to my left a plumbing vent jutted out from the shingles. Once there, I could use it to hold onto for a moment and then, with the pipe as an emergency anchor point beneath me, climb another twelve feet to the ridge line. From there it would be easy to cross over above my brother and slide down onto the toe board he was about to set in place on the angled irons. I'd save myself the time and trouble of climbing down the tree and then back up the ladder to reach the same place.

But the vent pipe was clear of the tree. There would be nothing to catch me if I failed to make it to my anchor point—just an open stretch of slope with a two-story fall from the eave to the lawn below. Also, though the pitch wasn't unmanageably steep, the roof was rotten. The asphalt shingles were dried out and had lost some, or perhaps most, of their grip on the tiny bits of gravel imbedded in them. Would my feet hold or would I slip instead like a man trying to walk on marbles?

Why did I, why would anyone, take an avoidable risk knowing full well that serious injury or death was more than just possible? The answers depend on who you ask—the death wish, karma, an unhappy childhood, testosterone levels, the evolutionary drive, machismo, adrenalin and endorphins, free will and predestination, "because it is there"—all reasonable but partial explanations, none of them quite satisfactory. The truth, it seems, is in the question itself; the answers, as usual, are false.

There isn't much difference between physical danger and psychic peril. An essay, done in the security of my chair, doesn't seem less dangerous than climbing a roof. The word is, after all, derived from the French *essai,* "a trial or attempt." Having spent years of my life constructing both houses and essays, I know that the emotional effect, fear and excitement, is the same with each. Lawrence Ferlinghetti recognized this in his poem, "A Coney Island of the Mind."

"Constantly risking absurdity/ and death/ whenever he performs/ above the heads/ of his audience/ the poet like an acrobat/ climbs on rime/ to a high wire of his own making…"

The lines between skilled and unskilled labor, between skilled labor and craft, between craft and art, become uncertain at times. It's largely a matter of attitude, of approach. Every good craftsman aspires to art and every good artist takes risks—the better the artist, the bigger the risks.

The practical kinesthetic art of the steeplejack was as necessary as the art of the architect in creating the cathedrals of Europe. One drew lines on paper; the other sat, hammer in hand, atop the spire. Without the architect it could not have risen, without the roofer it could not have lasted. Both, sustained by faith, took risks, and both, through grace, succeeded wonderfully well.

Of course, a cathedral, an essay, or any creation doesn't spring forth full blown. It's an orderly process. It starts with things as they are, the conditions at hand. Then you must see, clearly, what can be there and from that how to bring it about—foundation, walls, windows, buttresses, roof and spires.

From what is, the desire for what is not; out of the chaos of desire: a vision, then faith, courage and grace. Each step depends on the one before. No grace without courage, for fear makes us stumble. No courage without faith; no faith without a vision to believe in; no vision without the desire; no desire without something that already is which has the potential to change.

There's something odd about us humans that we can escape for a while our own mediocrity and do the work of angels—or of demons. How marvelous and terrible that we have the capacity for creation and destruction on an inhuman scale. No matter what we try, or why, we meet fear—and then we do something about it.

I stood on a tree branch and wanted to step onto the roof and climb to the ridge line. I saw the route from where I stood, across to the vent pipe and up to the ridge. I could feel in my body the swift smooth steps before I took them. It simply remained to be done.

I dropped my handsaw down to the lawn and drew a breath while rehearsing the movement in my mind. That done, I began. One step and I'd left the tree. Two more and I was about halfway to the vent. On the third step though, my foot slipped a little and I paused, unsure of my footing. Had I kept going, I probably would have made it, but a moment's hesitation, a quick glimpse into the uncertain future instead of paying attention to the present, was enough to fall in.

Without my momentum, the loosely held gravel of the shingles gave way and I found myself sprawled face-down and sliding, feet first, toward the eave. I quickly slid a couple of feet before I could slow myself by spreading out my arms and legs and relaxing my muscles. In the jargon of physics, I was altering the coefficient of friction between myself and the roof by increasing the amount of surface area contact—though, at the time, force vectors were not much on my mind.

"Tom!" I shouted. "I'm slipping. Bring the ladder!"

"What are you doing?" my brother asked. But I wasn't in the mood to explain to him how I'd gotten in that situation.

"Just bring the ladder. Hurry!"

I could see the vent pipe above me and hear my brother's feet ringing on the rungs as he scooted down the ladder. A quick blow with a hammer might have sunk the head through the roof and given me something to cling to, but I'd left it with my tool belt on the lawn when I climbed the tree. I tried to dig my right foot into the shingles in preparation for a dash for the vent, but couldn't get any purchase.

Now what?

I needed to know how much roof I had left before I slipped over the edge. Rolling over carefully, I managed to turn onto my back. I was still slipping, slowly and inexorably, but at least I could see what was coming.

It's amazing how much thinking you can do in a short time and with three feet left I had a plan—not much of one, but, given the circumstances, the only sensible one. If need be, I would fling myself outward from the eave at the last possible moment.

While loading a roof one frosty morning a few years before, my partner had dropped a bundle of shingles which immediately slid away toward the eave. Foolishly, he chased it down the roof and stopped it by tapping it with his foot. Though the bundle stopped, he didn't. He kept running right off the roof and down onto the lawn below, rolled across the grass and then stood up, unhurt. Luckily, it was only a short one-story fall for him.

This time, though, it was my misfortune to be sliding toward a tall two-story drop. Still, the principle was sound, partially overcoming gravity through angular momentum. The faster I moved away from the house, the less downward impact I would have when I hit the ground.

I kept rehearsing my leap in my mind as I slid toward the edge: push off with my feet, fling myself outward, try to get sideways with my head higher than my hips and feet, stay loose, tuck and roll as I touched the ground.

I was eight inches from the edge and steeling myself for the leap when the top rung of the ladder appeared directly beneath my feet with a soft metallic clang. My foot stopped against it and with a sigh of relief I rolled over onto my hands and knees and stepped down onto the ladder.

My brother was waiting for me at the bottom of the ladder. "You idiot! You could've got killed. What the hell were you doing up there? What, are you crazy?" he wanted to know.

I really had no explanation though, "I don't know... I just... blew it. I thought I could climb it. Thanks, man, you saved me."

"You're a fool's fool, dude," he muttered and shook his head wonderingly.

"Yeah, well... You're right," I admitted. "I had no business being out there. I just wanted to try it."

"Well, I guess we ought to take a break, huh?" he suggested.

We sat in the shade under the avocado tree for a while not saying much. I was embarrassed by my slip and my brother kindly dropped the subject. In fact, we've never talked about it since, though once in a while I remember and wonder about that morning and try to sort it all out.

It's obvious that I wasn't acting altogether sensibly,

but lately, I've taken to asking myself whether or not I would have slipped if I had been truly, wholeheartedly, foolish. If it was hesitation that made me slip, and if fools rush in because they have no fear, then perhaps I just wasn't foolish enough.

Red

$\mathcal{A}$ silver-haired old man sits in his mobile home in a trailer court and traces the still-fresh surgical wound on his chest with his finger. They told him, when he awoke in the Intensive Care Unit, that he'd died for a few minutes on the operating table. His ribs are still sore because the brittle bones cracked from the pounding it took to revive his failed heart. Time nearly stopped for him and continues now measured by the mechanically regulated beating in his chest.

"Your heart is enlarged," the cardiologist had told him, "like an athlete, or someone who has worked very hard for a long time."

Children play outside among the close-packed homes and cars and pickups lining the graveled court. He pauses for a moment and somewhere time breaks loose, drifting on tides of memory.

He is young, his hair red and thick again.

He is once again a boy in a logging camp, waking in the early dawn to check his trot lines left overnight in the river. A great sturgeon slowly rises to the shore, pulled in by straining boys.

At noon the clouds hang low as the child stands on a wooden dry flume, holding a brush and a bucket of grease. Thunder approaches and he clings to the side of the shaking flume as a log roars past on its way to the river below.

He is a guardsman on the Fourth of July. His cavalry troop waits in the square, mounted on freshly broken broncos pawing the dirt, waiting for the start of the parade. The brass band strikes up a march and suddenly the half-wild horses all bolt, snorting and leaping in terror, throwing their riders and scattering wild-eyed through the summer streets. The troopers brush off the dust from their uniforms and swear as they begin the chase.

He dances with a logger's widow at a country barn dance, his heart light with polka music and Prohibition whiskey. By the light of kerosene lamps they move across the wooden floor to the rhythm of fiddles, banjo and accordion. They near the open doorway and suddenly he leads her past the sawhorse plank table loaded with coleslaw and potato salad and lemonade, out into the warm summer night.

"Oh Red, what'll people think?" she asks, as they leave the lamplight behind for moonlight.

"Well, I don't know, but I'll betcha it ain't nothin' I ain't already thought," he replies and laughs.

Sitting in his narrow living room he laughs again at the telling then winces at the pain in his ribs. The sun shines down on the trailer court by the river and he smiles. "By God," he says, "we had some good times."

Work, Stubbornness and the Sweet Life

$\mathcal{O}$ne of the great difficulties in trying to understand the past is that people just don't work like they used to—long, hard hours of grueling stoop labor every day. Maybe that's a good thing. I can't honestly say that I wish I had the inescapable necessity of working like people did in my grandfather's day. I've done enough manual labor to guess at what it must have been like and can assure you that I'd rather be shifting a computer's cursor.

Bucking hay, for example, is not much fun. The bits of chaff and dust and grass seed cling to your sweating body, forming a gritty crust around your eyes as you bend and lift fifty-pound bales, stacking tons of fodder up in the hay loft. It is as stultifying to the mind as the thick hot air of the summer barn is to the lungs. And yet, there is something to be said for going to bed tired every night and waking up hungry.

My grandfather would have chuckled all winter if someone had told him, during some August afternoon harvest work break, that a multi-billion-dollar industry would someday be built by millions of people paying good money for the chance to sweat. "By the sweat of your brow…" Adam was told as he left the Garden. A curse, perhaps, but also a formula for health, as aerobics instructors and cardiac specialists will warn you.

Sickles made of bone and flint have been dug up by archaeologists at sites that date back to Neolithic times. For all those thousands of years, people dreamed of a golden time, in the mythic past, when the curse of hard work had yet to be laid on humankind. More recently, since the dawn of the industrial revolution with its mechanical gadgetry, the dream has shifted to the mythic future. It is a dream so old and so deeply embedded in human aspirations, that we almost never see it as a dream, but take it for an attainable goal.

But there is a loss that comes with our gain, one that shows up not just in cardiovascular diseases and diabetes, but in a loss of once common knowledge, a physical education which brings an outlook and attitude as well.

Getting the hay in is not just a matter of heat, sweat and grit. The work can't be done alone. It is a task shared with others, a labor of love done by a family, and much more fulfilling than recreational "quality time" which requires no sacrifice except of money. Along with the unpleasant labor comes the security of a full barn, the assurance of having enough to make it through another winter, and the satisfaction of having done something useful.

"Misery" the old saying goes, "loves company." Shared misery, if it is physical and not emotional misery and necessary to achieve something useful, is the enactment of love. "Arbeit macht das Leben suss" was a proverb of my sod-busting pioneer ancestors and one which explains a lot about how they endured so much, so well, for so long. It means, "Work makes life sweet."

That's a proverb that is almost incomprehensible here in the United States where manual labor is considered an anachronistic evil. It's not the sort of slogan that sells kitchen gadgets, or movies, or beer—Madison Avenue's version of the sweet life. We are taught to avoid using our strong backs (the sign of a weak mind) and to purchase our leisure by working with the insubstantial, to deal in digits and information. Our system in fact rewards us for doing so. The less substantial and meaningful the work the higher the income we expect from it.

This attitude towards "grunt work" is a product of the industrial revolution. The labor-saving machines which promised to liberate us have changed the nature of work itself. For the modern laborer, both in the fields and in our factories, work seldom proceeds at the pace of bone and muscle and breath. Instead, the rhythms are those of machinery, a mindless rate which never pauses and never varies. When people are forced to keep pace with a machine, the machine doesn't learn to become more human, and so the worker struggles to keep from becoming mechanical and yearns for the chance to work intelligently and creatively.

I acquired an old treadle sewing machine once, as a Christmas gift for my wife. The finish on the oaken cabinet was darkened and cracked so badly that I couldn't see the wood grain and so I took it to my mother's house to refinish it in secret. "Oh, God, one of those old things," my mother sighed as I unloaded it onto the sidewalk. "I was so glad when we finally got electricity and my mom bought a motor for our sewing machine and I didn't have to peddle the damned thing anymore."

I was taken aback, to hear her talk of this soon-to-be lovely antique, but to her it was a reminder of all the drudgery she'd escaped, while to me it was an elegant artifact from a time when craftsmanship and handiwork were valued, a time when making things always required human muscle, human intelligence and human creativity.

I was foolish enough back then to think of those days as a simpler time. I know now that it just isn't so. Getting by in "the good old days" was neither more nor less complicated than it is today—just differently complex. What I yearned for, in my sentimental ignorance, was the old-time directness of purpose as opposed to the overwhelming confusion of modern life. It seemed to me then (and this turned out to be true) that it would be better to deal with real excrement than the metaphorical kind. I just never suspected that shoveling cow manure every day had its drawbacks too.

For five winters, I used to dread the first week of tree planting season. No matter what kind of labor I'd been performing over the summer, there was simply no way to be prepared for those November days back on the mountain slopes. My calves would start aching before the morning cigarette break of the first day. By lunch time the pain was unbearable, and four and one half more days stretched ahead before the first day off.

A night's rest was not enough to heal it. I'd awake with useless legs and hobble off to work, knowing that the next morning would be more painful yet. I'd make it through the second day only by reminding myself that as bad as it was, the third day—the real killer—was ahead. Thursday and Friday provided exhaustion and numbness, the promise of two days of rest and a sense of pride in having survived. Wednesday, Hump Day, provided only pain.

Each plodding step taken on the first Wednesday of the season was the last possible step, starting with the very first step of my desperate daily mile. Wednesday was when the pukers quit. Wednesday had neither a beginning nor an end, no future and no past, no laughter or tears. There wasn't even endurance anymore; there was only annihilation without transcendence. The hopeless world was reduced to one day-long eternal moment.

During the long rides through the mountains on our way home from work, we tree planters used to fantasize about opening a survival school for upper middle class people. The notion was to lure doctors, lawyers and college professors out into the brush for a week on the slopes by appealing to their liberalism and sense of adventure. We would promise to give their presumably empty lives meaning through noble and useful work healing the earth one seedling tree at a time—work which, of course, they would pay us handsomely for the chance to perform.

It seemed like an entirely plausible scenario. After

all, we were talking about people who embraced utterly alien concepts like health clubs, personal trainers, Outward Bound, jogging, recreational hiking, vegetarianism, and putting fur trappers and houndsmen out of work. Surely, with the right advertising, one could persuade their sort to pay a thousand non-refundable dollars or more each for the chance to attempt a wintery week-long Cascade mountain death march.

The fantasy was mostly sadistic but not entirely so. We longed for the chance to watch the privileged collapse under the strain of an average day's work, not just to laugh at their pain and humiliation, but on a deeper level, to be understood and respected.

Manual labor is a specialized field, one that most Americans would fail at, just as most of us wouldn't last long as NFL linemen or as neurosurgeons. It takes time, several years, and persistence to become a competent laborer because it is time spent in a search for a peaceful acceptance of pain. It is a difficult process, harder than digging up stumps, harder than grubbing rocks in the bottom of a well. In the end, the laborer comes to know pain intimately, in all its many forms, and to realize that life is always painful—and yet it is only pain.

The Money Road

Rock Old Woman

Morning fog lies thick on the south side of Sexton Mountain. It's an evil stretch of freeway, just north of Grants Pass, Oregon—steep, winding, often icy when other reaches of the road are clear.

It's been a bad stretch for a long time. Back before the first wagon train creaked and rumbled through here, the Takelman people visited a large boulder by the trade trail. Rock Old Woman, she was called. For a gift of salmon and acorns she'd lure your enemies to their deaths. One day they'd find themselves passing through and meeting up with an old woman, who offered to share a pipe of tobacco. One puff and they'd be captured. Sexton Mountain would then rise, tie his hair in a knot and beat them to death.

She's gone now, blasted into fragments and bulldozed aside to make room for four lanes of Interstate 5. The old Indian trail, the "Money Road," which led to the Columbia River where woodpecker scalps and obsidian were exchanged for dentalia-shell money, now bears a different, swifter traffic, though its purpose remains the same and this particular stretch still fools unwary people and claims their lives.

It makes me nervous to cross this pass where dense fog and silvery morning light leave me leaning foolishly toward the windshield of Frankenstein, my patched-together old pickup. I hesitate to turn on my headlights because they've been suffering from an erratic short circuit lately. This eight-hundred mile trip is planned to take two days, so that I can avoid driving by night. Still, in fog this dense, my white pickup is closer to invisible than I dare risk. The lights come on and I make the descent without any problems and shut them off again with a sigh of relief. I have no enemies it seems—or none at least who know the proper chants and the right gifts to offer. Fifty miles gone and 750 more to go.

Like so many of the seven million drivers who pass through here every year heading north or heading south, I need to find some work. I'm tired of waiting, of living on hope, of depending on other people.

Twenty years ago the wages for blue-collar workers in southern Oregon were as good, or better, than average. But that was then. Nowadays, they've fallen considerably and, I'll admit, I'm forty-five years of age instead of twenty-five and can't compete as easily for jobs with the young bucks as I used to. I know of only one place where I can find the combination of decent wages and suitable work that I need—eight hundred miles south in *El Pueblo de Nuestra Señora de Los Angeles,* aka: L.A. Three of my brothers are trade show installers down there and they tell me there's seasonal work for casual laborers.

Fast Freight

I came to Los Angeles to try to find work fourteen years before at this same autumnal time of year. The times were rougher then, more desperate. It was 1983 and everyone, it seemed, was out of work, though the statistics showed that the percentage of unemployed workers in southern Oregon was merely in the high teens. I left and came to the city, lured by the chance to work evenings in a warehouse in East L.A.

The daytime streets held desperate men, Guatemalans and Salvadorans fleeing Central American death squads, Mexican *braceros* hoping to send a few dollars home to their hungry mountain villages and squalid *colonias* on the edges of cities. They stood on the sooty sidewalk on certain corners, waiting for construction and landscaping contractors to pick a few of them up for a day of grunt labor and a few unreported twenty-dollar bills.

Every evening for two weeks I crossed the Southern Pacific railroad tracks and stood by the door of Superior Fast Freight hoping to earn eight dollars per hour by loading and unloading semi-trucks and boxcars. There was always a small crowd of perhaps twenty men waiting along the sloping concrete ramp that led upward to the door we hoped to pass through. Most of the men were Latinos, and each of us was, by our presence there, patently in need. We were a rough-looking bunch, somber faced, tattooed, a calloused and scared clump of laborers, winos and junkies leaning against the iron railing, glancing anxiously at the doorway, awaiting the hiring boss.

Night after night a young corn-fed white boy in his early twenties would appear, choose a few strong backs from among the crowd and then I, along with the rest, would shrug and wander off into the night. I worked one night and spent my homesick days looking for something else to do. On all but two of those nights (the one night I worked and on my last night outside the door) the routine never varied.

That last night the kid stepped through the door and surveyed the crowd with an amused expression. "Are you hungry?" he asked.

We glanced at each other, our sullen indifferent masks torn for a moment and then, our expressions more opaque than ever, turned to look at him standing there above us, blocking the doorway.

"I sure hope you're hungry," he went on, his mouth twisting into a grin, "because if you ain't hungry tonight you ain't workin'."

And what were we to say? It was self-evident that we were all desperate for work. Did he even want us to reply? The routine was broken, our roles somehow changed, the unspoken relationship now out there in the naked industrial light. Was this some sort of trick, a challenge perhaps, or was he merely toying with us, like a child pulling the wings from a fly? What did it mean?

No one responded.

A brief look of doubt crossed his face for a moment, as though some perverse secret longing had been revealed and unfulfilled. Somewhere in his soul, somehow he must have felt a pang of shame. And then his face hardened to match ours.

"Are you hungry?" he asked again, a demand this time and not a question. "Everybody who's hungry raise your hands. Come on, raise 'em up! I want to see who's really hungry here tonight."

No one moved. A few turned to their neighbors and softly translated his words into Spanish.

The punk deserved a beating. You can't humiliate a workingman and expect to cow him with mere words. But we were no longer simply men. We were our families also. We were the need of our wives and children who did not witness our shame but who waited at home counting on us to provide what this young bully's nod could either allow us or withhold—a chance to earn our daily bread. We'd come, night after night, to try and salvage the pride we'd already lost. We had only the thin illusion of pride, and now even this small luxury must be surrendered if those we loved were to survive.

One by one, we all averted our eyes and raised our hands like docile schoolchildren asking our teacher's permission to go to the restroom. He smiled then, pleased with himself, chose a half-dozen laborers from among us and walked back through the door without another word.

What Passes

After five weeks down in Los Angeles the Fall trade show work dried up with nothing much doing until January. I left for home on a Friday afternoon, out the 210 Freeway to I-5 in the San Fernando Valley with fifteen hundred dollars mailed home to the good and a hundred bucks in my pocket. With any luck I'd be home by Saturday afternoon, two easy seven-hour runs: from The City of Angels to Sacramento, overnight in the Big Tomato, and then north to the One Hundred Valleys.

I'd hoped to make more money and expected to stay longer. But hope doesn't pay the bills, work does, and there was no sense in staying away any longer. Things looked good for January and February and perhaps March too—if I could put up with homesickness and alienation that long. And it was good to be heading home, to my wife and son, to my place, and to "my craft or sullen art."

Old Frankenstein, my reanimated corpse of a pickup, cobbled together from a half-dozen junkyard rigs, hummed along nicely for the first twenty-five miles. I was climbing the grade up the Grapevine, singing Reverend Spooner's version of Saul Pimon's "Bomeward Hound," when Frank coughed, hesitated long enough to cost me five miles per hour, backfired sharply and lurched forward again. I worked the accelerator pedal cautiously and found that pressing it caused the engine to stall while letting up slightly allowed it to recover.

Cheap gas?

Plugged fuel line?

Carburetion?

Ignition?

Hubris?

Frank held his own for a while. I hoped it was just a freak occurrence, maybe something to do with chaotic systems theory, just the right combination of the wrong things, causing a temporary problem. He seemed to run fine downhill, picking up speed but then each upward grade brought the problem back. Each cough threatened to be his last gasp, each explosive backfire struck like the thunderbolt of an angry god.

The bedeviled pickup wouldn't run right and yet kept running. I stopped at the Gorman summit, at Grapevine on the San Joaquin side, Kettleman City, Santa Nella, and Los Baños, trying to exorcise the inexplicable demon. I blew out the fuel filter, tightened the carburetor screws, checked the choke, cleaned the distributor rotor, checked the plug wires. Each town I reached was a temporary triumph, each triumph was followed by a new, and perhaps unreachable goal: the next town up the road. Greasy and exhausted, I limped into Sacramento at forty-five miles per hour and in the morning changed the carburetor's float valve.

Woodland: Gunk-Out carburetor spray. Winters, Willows, and the truck falls into a steady pattern, four seconds of coughing and sputtering, followed by four seconds of smooth running. Williams, and a search for an open garage. No luck, it's Saturday.

Following a set of directions given to me by a kid in an auto parts store I find a farmhouse outside of Corning where his dad reads a diagnostic scope and tells me to try installing a new distributor cap, rotor and plug wires. I offer to pay him and he shakes his head and laughs, "Nah, forget it. Hell, you're having too much fun."

Back in town I buy the parts and install them in the parking lot outside the parts store. It does me no good. The mantra continues: "If only I can make it to Red Bluff. If only I can make it…" Then, one by one, I insert the name of the next town: "If only…" Redding,

Lakehead, Dunsmuir, Shasta City, Weed, Yreka.

Each sputtering mile is a tightrope walk of concentration, a delicate balancing act of finding and holding the right pressure on the gas pedal. Too much gas and it sputters, not enough and it slows down to a crawl. Somehow I adjust.

One by one, each pass is somehow climbed and each doubt-filled mile lies behind me: from California into Oregon over Siskiyou Summit; through the Rogue River country and over Sexton Mountain and Stage Road Pass; down the backside of Smith Hill and Canyon Mountain where the South Umpqua River flows. At last I come to our own little Orchard Valley, our graveled county road and then down our driveway, tired and worried still but home at last.

Paul's Test

The Old Timer usually isn't excitable but when I told him about urine testing and Ed Meese he nearly swallowed his chew. "Meese?" he asked and spat on the potbellied stove. "Piss tests…" he added meditatively and wiped his brown-stained chin with his shirt sleeve while the wood-burner hissed.

"Wonder if he's any kin to ol' Measly Meese? I reckon you heard a' Measly ain't you? Well, ol' Measly set up a piss test one time too. Hell of a deal, to make a grown man pee in a cup to keep his job. Why a man'd have to be lower than a snake's belly to ask something like that. 'Course he learnt better finally, the hard way you might say, when he come up against ol' Paul.

"See: Measly Meese never cared much for the workin' man. All he ever loved was his damned machines and his bank account. Oh he was a tight one, always complainin' about the cost of labor and the Wobblies, and tryin' to find ways to make more money—as if he didn't have more than enough anyways.

"Why, one time up at Lousy Camp, the boys wanted to put new shakes on the bunkhouse. They was holes in that roof you could stick your head through, and all they asked for was a keg of number six nails and some shake bolts to split up for roofin'. But ol' Measly wouldn't have none of it. 'Ain't nothin' wrong with that roof,' he says. 'Why my grampa laid them shakes, and if they was good enough for him, they're damn sure good enough for the likes of you.'

"Oh, he was a mean one, and I can't say as anybody ever cared much for him neither, but he owned half the county (mostly railroad land he got on the sly) and if a man was gonna work around here, why he worked for Measly Mr. Meese.

"It was ol' Measly that hired the whole engineering school up at the university and a regular bee-swarm of millwrights to build him the Tin Logger, that big ol' steam robot that was supposed to put us all out a work. Folks talked like it was Doomsday a comin' and I reckon it would a been too, for a lot of folks around here, if Paul hadn't a challenged the tin man to a logging contest and worked his iron heart to death.

"Everybody thought the world of Paul after that. They never was a logger like ol' Paul Bunyan, finest woodsman ever to lace up a pair of caulk boots—bar none. Measly couldn't afford to fire him so Paul teased the old man to no end. It got to where the ol' skinflint wouldn't come to camp anymore for fear of Paul remindin' him of the Tin Logger's untimely demise.

"And that's where things stood 'til Measly Meese got scientific about it and paid a college perfessor to invent a test for loggers. Now, everyone knows that a real logger pisses vinegar and this here perfessor figured out a way to test for that. A man 'ud pee in a cup and they'd stick a piece of paper in it and dependin' on the color it turned they could tell how good a logger a man was. If it turned blue then you was only fit for government work, pale blue for shopkeepers, and white for farmers. If it come out pink you might make a millhand but if it turned red, then you was a natural born logger, the redder the better.

"Now Meese was a crafty ol' booger, and he figured out a way to shame Paul by monkeyin' around with the test and makin' it look like Paul weren't no logger at all—the ol' switcheroo. See: Meese had a jug of politician's piss he'd bought up at Salem there—tested deep indigo blue—and he was gonna switch samples on Paul to make it look like he was as worthless as they come—scientific proof, see? He figured that with Paul out of the way he'd make everybody take the test and hire only real loggers after that and thereby improve production. He even figured he could break up the I.W.W. that way, by 'proving' that union men wasn't real loggers.

"Measly loaded up the phony jug and the perfessor and came upriver where we was workin' up at Toketee, where the falls is nowadays. We heard the dinner bell ringin' early and we all come into camp to see what was wrong. I rode in in Paul's shirt pocket and was right there when he come into camp. Ol' Paul lit up when he seen it was just Measly Meese come to camp and no real emergency.

"'Why, hell-o there Measly,' says Paul. (He was the only man ever dared call him that to his face.) 'How's ol' Turret Head doin'? I heard he's seen the light, done converted—to a boiler at the cannery! Is that right?'

And he laughed that big ol' laugh of his that come up like water from a spring. But Measly Meese just bided his time and didn't say nothin' 'til the rest of the men come in.

"'Well boys,' says Meese, 'I reckon you're wonderin' why I called you all in from your appointed labors and how come I brung this feller here.' And he points to the perfessor, a little guy with spectacles who stood there blinkin' like he never seen a bunch a dumb-ass choker setters and bullwhackers before. 'Now I always said I got the best damn bunch a loggers anywheres and the perfessor here's ready to prove it. I know how you all like to carry on about who's the Bull O' the Woods and who's a sod-buster in a logger suit. Well, the perfessor has a scientific test to prove once and for all who's a real logger and who ain't. So, from now on only real loggers is gonna work for my outfit. Any man who can't pass this test, or who refuses to take it, I'm gonna can right on the spot. I want only the best workin' for me. So line up and pee in the cup. We'll dip the paper in it and if it don't turn red, you're dead. It's all scientific and the perfessor here's gonna keep it all fair and square. The test don't lie so give 'er a try and we'll see who's who. You first Mr. Bunyan.' And they brung out a railroad water tank for Paul to fill up.

"Now Paul knew he was the best logger that ever lived and he weren't shy about it neither. He knew he could pass any test that was legit as he had been winning contests all his life. He could out-work, out-run, out-climb, out-eat, out-drink and out-spit any logger he'd ever met. But there was one thing he was shy about and that was relieving himself in public.

"See: as a young-un his folks had always told him to go far off from the house when nature called—and I don't blame 'em, do you? And when he got older, folks was naturally curious about the size of his organ, him bein' a giant and all, and he took a lot of ribbin' about it. So, what with one thing and another, he'd gotten into a life-long habit of bein' alone when the time come. (And I was always grateful for that, to tell the truth, for he was a powerful man and could raise a powerful stink too.) So, naturally, Paul picked up the water tank and was gonna walk off a ways with it to fill 'er up and bring it back. But Measly wouldn't have none of it.

"'Fair and square and scientific,' he says. 'I don't want nobody to have a chance to cheat.'

"Well, Paul called him every name in the book and a few that weren't even thought-up yet, but Measly kept insisting that it had to be on the up and up, so Paul finally had to give in. He was just too stubborn and proud to let any man (or even ol' Measly Meese, who wasn't really what you'd call a man) say that Paul Bunyan wasn't a real logger.

"'OK,' says Paul, 'we'll see who's who and what's what. Hope you brung your raingear Measly, 'cause you're gonna need it.' And he set the tank there on the ground and whipped out that big ol' whanger of his and everybody ran under the cookhouse porch roof for cover. Paul laughed to see us runnin' and turned his back dainty-like, to fill the tank.

"But it didn't do no good. Paul stood there and he tried. He talked to his member like it was a thick-headed mule but it refused to let go. He stood there an hour and then two. He cussed and pleaded, shook it and wrung it and tried everything he knew but still it wouldn't listen.

"Now this put ol' Measly in a bind, see: he couldn't say Paul was refusin' but he couldn't test him neither. Measly waited all day and all through the night but mornin' come and still the giant hadn't dripped a drop. Measly had an idea then and sent to town for beer, wagon loads of beer, and Paul tossed it down a keg at a time, one after the other. I never seen nobody—even Paul—drink so much beer. He drank Douglas County dry, then the whole state of Oregon and Measly had to send to San Francisco for more.

"Paul's binge went on for a month and a day like that, 'til he'd drunk the whole West Coast dry, from San Diego to Bellingham, and Measly was goin' broke from the bar tab. Oh, he was a mighty man, Paul was, and he had the mightiest thirst there ever was—but even Paul had his limits.

"Measly was downriver at the telegraph office orderin' a trainload of beer out of St. Louis when the high water hit and all the raingear in the world wouldn't a done him no good. In fact, back in them days the Umpqua was part of the Willamette but Paul loosed a flood that cut its own way through the coast range, sweeping ol' Measly Meese and his mill clean out to sea. It cut away the ground from under the camp too, left a big hole there where Toketee Falls is today. You know, I go up there sometimes to look at the falls and I always think of ol' Paul and how Measly never got to shame him with his dirty trick. By God, we had some fine times back then—damn shame it's all gone.

"Well, I don't know if this other feller is kin to ol'

Measly Meese or not, and of course Paul ain't around no more, so maybe the piss test is back to stay. I don't know, but I'll let you in on somethin': you don't have to be a giant just to stand up to somebody—lots of folks who knew right from wrong have done it over the years and they weren't no bigger than you nor me."

One Thousand Times a Day

$\mathcal{T}$he Arbor Day Foundation sent me a Tree Survey a few months ago. At least it said it was a survey but it turned out to be a pitch for donations in the form of a questionnaire. Still, I decided to finish reading the thing before I tossed it in the wood burner with the other junk mail. Living as I do in a southern Oregon forest, I found questions like "Are trees important to you?" amusing.

Reading along, I came to a question that gave me pause: "Have you ever planted a tree?" I thought first of the 150,000 trees that I planted while reforesting clear cuts in the Cascades and Coast Range of Oregon, about enough to cover three hundred acres of mountain slopes. That sounds like more than what it was though—after all, I have friends who were serious tree planters. My pal Darlene told me that she must have planted about a half-million of the little things during her winters on the slopes. And there are three of my ex-tree planter buddies—Johnny Escovido, Bruce Gordon and Les Moore—who slammed over one million trees in the ground apiece. I'm sure there are others among my acquaintances who have surpassed that impressive number but most tree planters don't talk about how many trees they've planted. They talk about their chronically sore backs.

One million trees sounds like a bigger deal than what it actually amounts to. It only takes about forty seconds to plant a seedling conifer eight feet away from the last one you planted. Reforestation crews generally plant about 500 seedlings to the acre, so a million trees would only replant about 2,000 acres of logged-off land, about enough to provide habitat someday for a single nesting pair of northern spotted owls. I've worked on corporate clearcuts here in Oregon that were that big while up north in British Columbia there are cuts that are measured in square miles rather than acres.

A few weeks later, I ran across Lester "The Rat" Moore and I got to wondering about when and where he planted his one-millionth tree. He was busy stealing firewood off of some timber company land at the time, buzzing up an old buckskin-colored seasoned madrone log and tossing the rounds into his pickup to haul back to the tar paper shack he lives in. He was in a hurry, and I was on my way into town, so we "howdied" but didn't stop to talk.

The Rat isn't exactly the sort of guy you'd see in a TV commercial. He's not the square-jawed handsome woodsman type the corporations like to show, nor the soft caring sort who serve as poster children for Arbor Day celebrations. He's a small, wiry, snaggly-toothed guy who chews tobacco and drinks his whiskey straight from the bottle. If you saw him on a city street you'd probably try your best to walk past him without making eye contact. He's not much of a hero, but when it comes to tree planting he was the genuine article—a steady 1,000 good trees every day, five days per week, twenty to thirty weeks per year for sixteen years.

It's a tough way to earn a paycheck, humping up and down mountains in the rain all winter. The State Employment Office in Eugene, Oregon, once posted a warning notice about tree planting: "It is the hardest physical work known to this office," it read. "The most comparative physical requirement is that of a five mile cross-mountain run, daily." Most people would consider logging a tough job; tree planting is a logger's idea of hard work.

That one-millionth tree of his career might have been planted in Oregon, or Washington, Montana, Idaho, British Columbia, Alaska, Arizona or Colorado. I doubt he remembers it. It was probably a lot like the twenty thousand others he planted that month and I'm sure that nobody handed him a golden shovel or took his picture for the occasion.

Nobody gives out awards for stoop labor, which is really a shame. It is difficult work, demanding both physically and mentally. I have seen many a fine physical specimen give up the attempt after a day or two because they lacked the necessary gumption (or the desperation, which is just as useful) to see it through to payday. Yet, the people who actually bend down and touch the earth in order to do the work of healing the world are always the least honored of all.

Grandmother's Earth

She stands, an old woman surrounded by herbs and flowers, in her front yard. Her house is small and old. The roof sags and the paint hangs in sad flakes like a molting chicken's feather. Her porch is cluttered with earthenware pots and with gardening tools whose worn edges have no rust and whose handles are smooth and dark and polished from use.

She feels the morning sun warming her bones and quietly utters a prayer: "Thank you Grandfather Sun for warming us all. Thank you for giving us your smiling face every day."

Her neighbors think she's a little bit dotty, muttering to herself and staring at an old oak tree on the edge of her property. But she remembers how her mother used to stand in the mornings, after her father, cussing and spitting tobacco juice, led the jangling mules to the fields. In the sudden peace he'd left behind him, her mother would stand, quietly, listening and staring out across the red clay hills of Oklahoma with those dark brown eyes that seemed to always take in more than they reflected.

One day she'd asked her mother what she was listening to when there was nothing to hear but the wind in the grass. "Everything has a voice if you listen close," she said, "trees and flowers and even the rocks, but you got to be quiet to hear 'em—real quiet." And she hadn't understood.

It was in the spring, and that summer the corn turned brown and died before it got more than knee high and the red dust was everywhere. And one morning her father sat on the porch and cursed the rising sun and the parched earth.

Her mother stood at the screen door and heard him. "You shouldn't a done that John," she said softly. "You went and cussed the land and now it won't give us nothin' no more."

"Don't talk like that, woman. It gives me the willies. You sound like your crazy squaw grandma. Don't you be wishin' no bad luck on me—I've had a belly full already."

"You done it yourself, John. You're bringing it on all of us. You shouldn't a cussed the land like that."

That was the summer the big storm blew in and the rain cut the dry fields up into deep gullies. That was the summer she understood what her mother meant about listening, the summer before they moved to Oregon.

Conrad and Me

$\mathcal{I}$ never would have gone beyond my GED if I hadn't taken up writing. I always loved literature and read constantly for pleasure. I enjoyed writing but avoided publishing it for years, out of fear of failure.

When I finally decided to risk an attempt at becoming a professional writer, in 1979, I floundered at it for a year, dabbling at it but not really working in the way I'd learned to persist at manual labor. Looking back on my first year's efforts—a handful of incomplete short stories—I decided to get some help and enrolled in an adult-education night class. I knew from experience that someone who knew more than me could show me useful things in a few minutes that I might spend years trying to learn through trial and error.

It was in the dead of winter and I was getting up at four A.M. to plant trees all grueling day and taking the class one night a week. Despite my exhaustion I came home wired on class nights, unable to get to sleep for a few hours. I didn't actually learn much about the craft of writing but my teacher encouraged me to keep at it.

I didn't get serious about writing though until the

following October when I fell (ten feet, head first) into it. A ladder twisted out from beneath me and, like Alice down the rabbit hole, I was pitched into a bewildering world of unavoidable chronic pain and systematic humiliation—the worker's compensation system.

For the first time in my life I was unable to work. It is hard, after years of defining yourself through pride in your body's strength and endurance, to find yourself disabled. Poems are written about athletes whose careers are cut tragically short by injury or death but a laborer who gets crunched on the job is merely categorized as a "flake" and discarded.

I was told to get minimum-wage work pumping gasoline but I turned to my manual typewriter for solace and challenge instead. It was a new world to compete in but I felt sure that hard work and stubborn persistence would eventually pay off in my literary labors as it had in the woods and mills and construction sites. (Like so many notions in my life this one turned out to be correct but terribly naive.)

I bought a ream of 16-lb. bond paper and decided that when I'd used up those 500 sheets I would be a writer. I wrote daily, journal keeping and trying my hand at short fiction. In my first six months I used up less than 200 sheets of paper though and had only three finished short stories to show for my efforts.

I applied for a tuition waiver to go to a writer's conference down in northern California and to my surprise it was granted. I had submitted a short story about a derelict who casually claimed to be (and may or may not have been) God. The conference participants were to be broken up into groups and would read copies of each other's work and spend an hour apiece in group critique sessions. Well-known writers would be on hand for workshops and to lead the groups.

It was an awkward week for me. I wasn't used to being around people who talked about literature. In one of the sessions someone commented on something being "like Garp" and a dozen participants nodded assent while I sat wondering who this Gorp guy was and what he had written. I thought maybe he was one of those nineteenth-century Russian novelists. Gogol, I'd read, as well as Dostoyevsky, Turgenev and Tolstoy—but Gorp?—never heard of him, though he must have been important since everyone else understood the reference.

My own story came up for its critique at the end of the week and was politely trashed by the group leader, a college professor and editor of a literary journal.

Authors, I was told, had no place within the story itself. Good fiction consisted in concealing one's personal beliefs and making your point only by showing what could be directly observed. Joseph Conrad himself, I was told, had endorsed this cinematic approach when he wrote, "My role as a writer is to make people see."

I'd never heard anything of the sort before and I assumed that I had failed and would continue to fail until I had learned the things that my fellow aspiring writers had learned in school while I was busy working. After all, here was a highly educated man, a Doctor of Philosophy and an editor who apparently was on a first-name basis with dozens of literary giants, and he was quoting from an author I deeply respected. I became determined to attend college and find out who

Gorp was and to learn everything else that these people had as an edge over me.

In September I enrolled in an English composition class at my local community college. I was amazed at the number of affluent-looking young women and young men walking around the place. It was strange to be among people whose hands were soft and pink and still had all of their fingers. Through all those years of toiling in the gritty, violent all-male world of stoop labor, I never knew (or even wondered) where well-dressed unscarred young people spent their days.

The conference had given me my first chance to size up the competition because, unlike manual labor, writing is done in isolation, which makes it impossible to glance over your shoulder and keep an eye on your fellow workers.

Here in Writing 121, I found that I alone among the thirty students knew or cared about our culture's literary traditions. I saw students carrying the *Norton Anthology* and heard them grumble about studying it. When I opened its covers I was shocked to find it full of short excerpts from the books I'd happily read in full—a chapter from *Gargantua*, a few pieces from the King James Bible, a handful of stanzas from Virgil's *Aeneid*. This was considered an education by the teachers and an excruciating burden by their frowning students. And Garp, I learned, was an improbable character in a trendy novel.

The teacher was a newly minted PhD who spoke of his doctoral exam as "the most terrifying experience that one can ever go through." I thought of an LSD-crazed biker named Stretch and a dicey night I'd spent stuck with him in a remote adobe in the mountains of New Mexico, the only time in my life I sincerely believed in demonic possession. Those oral exams must really be hell, I decided.

The prof spoke of writing as a terrible lonely struggle. Writing his doctoral thesis (on Joseph Conrad, it turned out) had nearly overwhelmed him and he'd barely managed to cobble it together with scissors and paste. Even though he'd earned his doctorate and gotten a good paying job as the head of the Humanities Department, I felt sorry for him. Why bother to write, I wondered, if you don't enjoy it? But he never spoke of having fun, only of relentless struggle and in the end, dissatisfaction.

I did my work faithfully, kept a journal for the class and turned in my assignments, but as the semester went on I began to doubt the usefulness of it more and more. One day though, I was shaken when he, in turn, quoted Conrad's dictum. For a moment all the shame and despair of that morning at the writing conference came flooding back. It seemed true after all—this stuff really was available only to those who could afford college tuition and I'd probably never make the grade as a consequence.

"As Joseph Conrad once wrote, 'My role as a writer is to make people see,'" the learned doctor told us, and for a moment my heart sank.

"But, of course," he added, "he meant that in the moral sense—not visually."

Belonging

$\mathcal{I}$ remember going to a book club supper meeting about a decade ago. I'd never been to one before but I'd been invited to attend because the group's membership had read a book that I'd written and wanted to talk about it with me. Everyone was horribly nice to me, the meal was good eating and the literary conversation was downright stimulating at times. I should have been as happy as a politician at a $10,000 per plate fundraiser but I felt out of place among those gracious strangers.

In part, I was simply afraid that I might lapse into my habitual ways of speaking and offend them. It made me nervous to hear them speaking English correctly while I worked to hold back the colloquialism-laced dialect and ready profanity that I use when I relax among friends. These well-dressed and well-educated and well-meaning people were definitely not my friends. For one thing, none of my friends would ever join a book-discussion club.

It struck me then that if I hadn't written the book, none of these folks would have wanted to hang out with me, nor I with any of them. Under most other circumstances I probably would have regarded each of them, on first meeting, as mere "yuppie-fucks," to be distrusted and, if necessary, lied to as well.

A few of those earnest readers took exception to one of my essays in which I had opined that class prejudice was inevitable in our society and admitted my own ingrained prejudice against professional-class people. They seemed to truly believe that we live in a classless society here in America. I did my best to disillusion them in as kindly a fashion as I could muster, and the whole conversation was as polite and calm as anyone could wish for, but still, I felt their resentment, mild as it was, and felt bad about that. I would not willingly cause anyone to be unhappy and these were clearly very decent folks who didn't deserve to be upset by me or my writings.

I left there that night troubled, wondering where I had failed in composing that one essay in the collection that was being talked about, and feeling that the conversation about it hadn't gone well either. I really do try to be aware of my prejudices and to set them aside as much as I can, but it isn't easy to do so and I don't always succeed in catching myself in the act. As always, the feelings come first and the words to explain them only later and often only after months or years of pondering.

In looking into my generalized distrust of an entire class of my neighbors, it doesn't seem to be the obvious differences in wealth and power that immediately affect me so much as differences of speech which trigger my "flight or fight" response to doctors, lawyers, bankers, judges, politicians, college professors and social workers—anyone who has "colleagues." I cringe whenever someone uses "impact" to mean "effect" or "affect." When I hear "issue" being used to describe a problem, I have to hold myself back from barking out a hearty "Gesundheit!" I can fix a problem, but issues seem fuzzy, debatable, and abstract to the point of hopelessness.

I suppose someone with a different background than mine might find such vague and abstract talk amusing or annoying or a source of self-righteous contempt but, for me, it inspires actual fear. The vague words and empty phrases of nice people wouldn't bother me as they do if I didn't associate them with harm done—to me, my friends and family and my community—in the past.

Such language is not just irritatingly pretentious—it is also the vocabulary of oppression. It is the words your boss uses to lie to you, the language an insurance company uses to deny your claim, the vocabulary of the prosecutor who tries your case and of the judge who sentences you. It is the politician's tool of deception and demagoguery. It gives me the willies. I hear it and (to be honest) I think to myself, "Oh no! Here it comes—get out the Vaseline."

It is not that only one particular class of people harms others but a matter of degrees and types of harm. The crimes of the poor and of the uneducated are small in scale and personal in nature. The thief who steals my toolbox from the back of my pickup does me real harm, but it is personal harm, immediately known, measurable and limited in scale and duration.

The largest thefts and greatest crimes against humanity are never designed and set in motion by the powerless among us. I doubt that there were very many high school dropouts among those responsible for the recent collapse of our global economy. In fact, the primary players all seem to have graduated from our nation's most respected universities with advanced degrees and to have been receiving (I can't bring myself to call it "earning") extraordinary amounts of money in the process of putting tens of millions of Americans out of their jobs and their homes.

The crimes of the well-off and well-educated are impersonal, hidden, and, all-too-often, on a vast scale. These are qualities that, to me, are frightening. I'd much rather get mugged in a dark alley than to have myself, my family, my friends and my nation ripped off by faceless strangers working to increase corporate quarterly profits through unethical and illegal practices.

Fourteen years ago I was both pleased and a little ashamed to find at tax time that my wife and I had earned enough money to place us in the middle class. Twenty-six years of living in poverty and "working poor" near-poverty had become habitual and even, at times, a source of pride. A sense of pride is nearly as necessary to poor folks as are the physical necessities of food and shelter. After all, when your only wealth is your sense of self-worth, you cling to that for sustenance. When that pride is beaten out of us, all sorts of horrors follow: drug abuse, child abuse, domestic violence, divorce and suicide. Individuals, families and then whole communities break apart. Pride, honest pride and not the overblown sort that "goeth before the fall," won't show up on a spreadsheet but is more real and more important to our survival than the digits which represent the exchange of money.

It felt good, after all those years of hardscrabble getting by, to finally become "respectable." But it also felt as though we had entered enemy territory and that I faced the danger of becoming the sort of person I had scorned, someone soft and comfortable and cut off from the all-consuming daily struggle for existence of the poor. At heart, I think, it was something like survivor's guilt—the suspicion that somehow I didn't deserve the security that we'd finally gained—that left me uneasy with our newly earned status.

Each May for ten years in a row I worked on a crew setting up and tearing down a ridiculously large trade show booth for a giant corporation. One year, curious about just how big it really was, I asked and was told that we were installing fifty-six semi-truck trailer loads of material at an obscene cost to the company of $17 million for the three-day run of the trade show.

The booth setup took twelve days without a day off, and each day we worked from ten to twelve hours. Most of it was heavy work: lifting and carrying steel beams, installing a half acre of carpeting, hundreds of plywood panels, decking and railings, wall panels, doors, ventilation ducts and copper plumbing. It was hot and noisy and dangerous work and, of course, exhausting.

One year I stood two stories high atop the nearly completed project with the head electrician and watched the corporate "suits" and their young fresh-faced interns coming through on their annual pre-show tour.

"Here they come, Willie—look at them. Where do people like that come from anyway?" I wondered.

"Hell, it don't matter," Willie replied. "They've got their world and we've got ours and we like it just fine that way. We wouldn't like their world and they wouldn't like ours."

Embracing Opal Whiteley

*J*ust inside the door of the Cottage Grove Public Library there is a bronze statue of a young girl dancing joyously amid scattering leaves and adorned with block-lettered words taken from *The Story of Opal: The Journal of an Understanding Heart.* It is a lovely piece, a fitting monument to childhood itself as well as to the author who spent most of her childhood living near the town.

The book, an alleged childhood diary written at the age of seven, was published in 1920, and its author was most commonly known as Opal Whiteley. Those two facts are about all everyone seems to agree on in what became an Oregon literary controversy that continues to this day.

The library also houses a copy of an odd self-published book by the same author, *The Fairyland Around Us,* published in Los Angeles, California, in 1918. The book is fragile, kept in a cardboard box and wrapped in tissue paper to prevent damage. The title page gives the name of Opal Stanley Whiteley for the author and inside the front cover are a few browned newspaper clippings. The clippings deal with efforts to establish the authenticity of *The Story of Opal* and a report that Miss Whiteley had been recently spotted in Udaipur, India, riding like a princess in a royal carriage with a military escort.

On September 24, 1919, Opal Whiteley met with Ellery Sedgewick, editor and publisher of *The Atlantic Monthly* at his office in Boston. The *Atlantic* had recently started publishing books and Opal brought a copy of her self-published *The Fairyland Around Us* in the hope of selling it to The Atlantic Monthly Press. Mr. Sedgewick wisely declined to publish Opal's uneven hodgepodge of a book but asked about her childhood diary, which she had mentioned in her cover letter requesting an appointment. Opal told him that she still had the diary but that it had been torn to pieces by a younger sister and that the fragments were stored in Los Angeles, where she had been living while writing her first book. The diary fragments were sent for and Opal spent the next several months supported by Sedgewick while she worked on producing a manuscript from the reassembled pieces. It appeared during 1920 in installments in *The Atlantic* which were later published as *The Story of Opal.*

Opal Irene Whiteley was what her parents named her. She was also known as Opal Stanley Whiteley, Françoise d'Orlé, Marie de Bourbon, Francesca Henriette Marguerite d'Orléans, Françoise Marguerite Henriette Marie Alice Léopodine d'Orléans, and Françoise Marie de Bourbon-Orléans. But when people argue about who Opal Whiteley really was they tend to talk about one or another of three seemingly disparate Opals: Opal "The Sunshine Fairy," Opal the Fraud and Crazy Opal.

The debate usually involves someone emphasizing one or another of those three aspects of her life and personality and downplaying or denying the others. It is probably impossible to settle for once and forever all the many claims and counter arguments concerning who she was, what she did or didn't do and, especially, why. What is certain is that she created a memorable character—the little Nature Girl now immortalized in bronze—one that still appeals to a great many readers.

She was born in Colton, Washington on December 11, 1897, the eldest of Charles Edward Whiteley and Mary Elizabeth Scott-Whiteley's four daughters and a son. Ed Whiteley worked in the woods and in backwoods lumber mills. Back then, as now, it was hard work and it was seasonal work in a boom-or-bust industry and periodic layoffs were inevitable. As with so many families at the time, the Whiteleys were forced to move frequently in search of employment. Late in 1902 they left Colton, Washington for Wendling, Oregon, a hamlet near Marcola in the southern Willamette Valley. Two years later, at the time described in *The Story of Opal,* they were living near her mother's parents in Walden, another wide spot in the road located about four miles east of Cottage Grove.

The family lived at times in shoeless poverty but her cultural life was richer than one might expect, given the family's financial instability. Her parents were literate and her mother often read stories and poetry to the children and provided them with music lessons. Her childhood took place in the first decade of the twentieth century in a gritty Oregon that was still depending on horses and mules, a landscape and society richly described in the novels of James Stevens and H.L. Davis. She was a highly intelligent, imaginative, lively and precocious child full of questions and given to daydreaming, much like the Opal of her 1920 book. Her father, Ed Whiteley, doted on her and she must have been a charming little girl.

It is the details of that childhood, as portrayed in *The Story of Opal,* that are endlessly argued over. The details of landscape, many of the people and at least one of the incidents mentioned in the book have been verified by researchers. Other details are simply too fantastic for most people to swallow. The most unbelievable aspect is that the book contains a great many French words and a slathering of heavy-handed clues indicating that little Miss Whiteley was actually the orphaned daughter of French aristocrats—though she herself claimed to be unaware of that until several months after her book appeared.

Looked at from a literary view, *The Story of Opal* reeks of artifice. It is not a diary but a novel in diary form, beginning with an introductory chapter and ending with a dénouement and employing stock plots, foreshadowing, chapter finales and a blatantly disingenuous world view clearly designed to appeal to adult sensibilities. It belongs to an identifiable genre—nineteenth century mawkish stories of childhood such as Martha Finley's Elsie Dinsmore novels which feature an oppressively sweet-tempered little girl who is constantly running into parental trouble by being so very earnestly good.

John Steinbeck once pointed out that every novel contains a character who is the author's wished-for self. This imagined self is who we read about in *The Story of Opal*. It is probable that Opal Whitely really was a sensitive child, attuned to the great beauty of the natural world in imaginative ways that amounted to a sort of primitive and instinctual mysticism. She may well have known trees whom she regarded as friends and likely had a great fondness for animals and flowers.

Literature does not appear suddenly and fully realized out of nothing, but rather comes from within the author, drawn up in memory buckets from the well of experience. She could not have written as she did without being, to a considerable extent, the person she portrayed. Nor would the character she made of herself have appealed so strongly to so many without the readers' recognition of the underlying artistic truths contained within the novel and within themselves.

The strong appeal of Opal the character (as distinct from Opal Whiteley the author) explains a great deal about why modern readers in Britain and the United States still feel strongly enough about this book to defend its author on blog sites and in panel discussions. Skeptics and true believers alike may yearn for someone like Little Miss Whiteley with her unsullied outlook and mystical relationship with the natural world and with God. Opal's defenders, who call themselves "Opalites," fall in love with the self-portrait of this sweet little girl and, loving her, seek to defend her from her critics. Those critics are often overly dismissive of the book and its author because it has been promoted as an actual diary. This critical vehemence, in large part, may come from a feeling of betrayal because Opal, as "The Sunshine Fairy" character, is so seductively innocent and has such a great appeal that one can be fully aware of the deception and still want to believe in such a delightful creation.

Opal Whiteley's story is commonly promoted as a mystery. Mystery is a wonderful word, one that reliably sells books and magazines and provides gainful employment for publishers, editors and writers. In the matter of *The Story of Opal*, the mystery is not really whether or not the author misrepresented her manuscript but what her state of mind was at the time.

Opal had a photographic memory and drew attention at an early age by reciting long passages from the King James Bible. She took a strong interest in botany and wildlife biology and, from her studies, could name hundreds of species of plants, animals and insects by both their scientific and common names.

At the age of twelve she met G. Evert Baker, a Portland area lawyer who was lecturing in Cottage Grove on behalf of Junior Christian Endeavor, a religious social organization for adolescents. He urged Opal to start her own local chapter of the group and recruited her as an organizer. A few years later she was touring the state, charming large crowds and rapidly increasing the number of Junior Christian Endeavor chapters. In the process she learned about the value of self-promotion and she learned to rely upon the kindness of the strangers who fed and sheltered her. These two lessons became key survival strategies that served her well in her life.

In 1915, at the age of seventeen, she came to the attention of the press. Both the *Eugene Daily Guard* and *The Oregonian* ran stories about her, depicting her as a backwoods autodidact and genius who had almost inexplicably accumulated an encyclopedic knowledge of natural history. Actually, she had been attending school since the age of five, and was in high school at that point and, through the Oregon State Library, had read extensively on natural history subjects. But the reporters, as was all too common at the time, weren't about to let facts get in the way of a good story.

The press attention that year came when she visited the University of Oregon during a week-long stay with her aunt in Eugene and caused a stir among the faculty with her apparently encyclopedic knowledge of geology, wildlife biology and botany. Professor Warren D. Smith, head of the university's geology department at the time, declared, "She may become one of the greatest minds that Oregon has ever produced." Plans were put forth to waive the school's requirement that students complete high school and to give Opal a full scholarship. In the end she had to wait a year while she completed her senior year of high school and was admitted in the fall of 1916 with a small partial scholarship. Her college career lasted two years, during which she managed to complete about a year's worth of studies before dropping out due to poverty and time-consuming family crises.

She was clearly ambitious (she left Oregon in 1918 for Hollywood and a hoped-for career in the movies) and she was also clearly suffering from mental health troubles. As a teenaged lecturer and as a young woman she was said to have been plagued by nightmares and to have complained of being followed by shadowy figures. Between 1916 and 1922 she had four recorded episodes of what were called "nervous breakdowns." Each of these lasted several months and each came following months-long periods of extremely intense work—long days and overnight sessions running on little more than nervous energy.

Somewhere along the line she developed an *idée fixe,* believing that she was actually the orphaned daughter of Henri d'Orléans, a French nobleman and nineteenth century explorer and naturalist who died in 1901. She must have needed that story very badly. Somehow it helped her to understand herself and her place in the world. William Kittredge once wrote that much of what we struggle with as humans is the development of an evolving story about ourselves that allows us to make sense of our lives. Some of these stories are healthy stories that help us to survive; other stories are unhealthy stories. All of these stories are necessary responses to life's experiences.

Opal was acknowledged as exceptional while still a pre-teen—exceptionally intelligent, exceptionally knowledgeable and an exceptionally charismatic public speaker. At least adults saw her that way, although she seems to have been something of an outcast among her school mates. It is a wonder that anyone ever survives adolescence with its hormonal rollercoaster rides and doubt-filled search for a sense of self in a seemingly endless time of substantial physical, emotional and social-role changes. An exceptionally talented and socially awkward girl experiencing the effects of bipolar disorder might understandably find an exceptional explanation for why she found her life as it was.

Through her nature studies Opal Whiteley was familiar with the long-since discredited nineteenth century genetic theories underlying both Eugenics and Social Darwinism. A century ago many mainstream scientists, as well as celebrities such as Oliver Wendell Holmes and Andrew Carnegie, believed that moral inclinations, character traits and intelligence were unavoidably inherited just like one's hair color. If she felt superior to those around her (and she was told repeatedly that she was) and wondered at the reason for that, then being the orphaned daughter of European aristocrats, rather than being an Oregon logger's daughter, offered an attractive explanation. Eventually it might also have explained her nightmares (the result of childhood kidnapping trauma) and those unsettling feelings of being followed by unseen strangers (agents hired—sometimes for her good and sometimes harmfully—to keep an eye on the orphaned princess.)

It seems to have taken a few years to fully develop the story of her ancestry. During her time as a student at the University of Oregon, she told a local woman that she was an orphan. A few years later, in Los Angeles, she was saying that she had been born in Italy. By 1918 when she arrived in Boston, her story had become that of a French orphan.

It would be difficult to say to what degree Opal Whiteley believed in her increasingly elaborate story of marriage at the age of four to the Prince of Wales, shipwreck, kidnapping, being carried from Rome, Italy to Portland, Oregon, and being placed in the care of Ed and Lizzie Whiteley. Her frequent and almost casual fabrications concerning her life show that she was no stranger to deception, but the fact that she stuck to the story for the rest of her life seems to show that she actually believed it. Still, people sometimes intensely believe their own lies and an imaginative person playing a role long enough can virtually become the character they started out portraying. For many years beginning in the early 1920s, Franziska Schanzkowska, a Polish woman who went by the name of Anna Anderson, claimed to be Grand Princess Anastasia of Russia. She too seems to have believed her own story.

Opal was institutionalized in 1948 after her neighbors in London complained to the authorities that she'd been shouting in the street and that she was living in squalid conditions. She was diagnosed as having "paraphrenia with paranoid features." Paraphrenia is usually interpreted nowadays as a late-onset form of schizophrenia that typically appears at about forty years of age, though at the time it had a broader definition and served as a general term for delusional disorders that begin in middle age. Paranoia is of course, a common feature of schizophrenia but it is also sometimes associated with bipolar disorder.

She spent the last forty-four years of her life in

a British mental institution, growing increasingly paranoid. She believed herself imprisoned and by the early 1970s came to believe that Jews from outer space were masquerading as people she knew and planning to invade Oregon.

Those who condemn her often see the diary as a coldly fraudulent hoax. Some of her defenders insist that no fraud at all occurred while others conclude that the fraudulence was only partial and those parts excusable on the grounds that the author was mentally unstable. Reconciling the positive and negative aspects of Opal Whiteley's life and her art is difficult and painful for many readers. That someone as enticing as "The Sunshine Fairy" was also a liar and a moocher who hurt her own family deeply by denying her parentage is, understandably, too difficult for some readers to accept. But to ignore the harm she brought and focus only on the beauty she created does a disservice to her, to literature, to history and to Oregon.

It has been ninety-five years now since the day Opal Irene Whiteley kept her appointment with Ellery Sedgewick. My guess is that she was seeking not just a book deal but acceptance of herself as well. In the near century since that day neither those who condemn her for her fraudulence nor those who canonize her as a saint have managed to grant her the unconditional approval she so desperately sought.

Epilogue—Beautiful Dreamers

A station wagon pulling a trailer filled with furniture and packed cardboard boxes comes in to town from the Interstate. The driver and her husband take in the brick storefronts, the dress of the people, the surrounding hills, and, following a sign, come to the park. They are a little tired of driving and of watching the world through a bug-splattered windshield and pull over to rest.

The kids jump out and roll in the grass and their parents stand and stretch and look around carefully, not out of fear but with caution bred of hope and disappointment. It is a beautiful place compared to where they've come from, but they measure it against something else, something not quite distinct but which they've hungered after for a long while.

It is a dream which brought them here and it is that dream which they are comparing the place to. "Could this be it?" their eyes ask. They want it to be but are reluctant too, because they've seen many places and none were quite what they'd set out for.

"It's pretty isn't it?" she says.

He looks at the place, takes in the baseball diamonds, the soccer field, the band shell and the leafy trees along the shaded creek. An old couple is walking by hand in hand. Three boys tote fishing poles and bait boxes on their way to the river. A young man tosses a Frisbee to a black Labrador retriever who snatches it out of the air with his jaws.

"Yes," he admits, "it's nice."

Their children rush off toward the creek and they follow, walking slowly to the picnic benches, lost in thought.

There is so much they are trying to balance in their minds: worries about their supply of money and how much time they have left to choose and wonder about places they haven't looked at yet. It is hard to choose a place to settle down in when there are so many possibilities. It had seemed so much simpler at first, far away in another place, in another life—so much brighter and hope-filled. And now, there is the fear of making the wrong choice and the desire for something to come along, some sign to point the way for them. They were excited at first by all the choices, but now it seems they are growing weary of it and yearn to be free from freedom itself.

"Yeah," he says, "it's nice here. Let's spend the night and take a look around tomorrow, check the place out."

By the same author:

OVERSTORY: ZERO
REAL LIFE IN TIMBER COUNTRY
2nd Edition

Robert Leo Heilman's award-winning essay collection about work, family, community, and the land is back in print, revised and expanded with ten new pieces added about small-town life in timber country.

"This is a huge short book. Better than anyone but Ken Kesey, Robert Heilman writes how woods and streams shape a working people. He just nails it."
—Robin Cody,
author of *Ricochet River* and *Voyage of a Summer Sun*

"Overstory: Zero serves a never-to-be-shaken blow against every cliché, redneck or tie-dyed, that has wrongly colored the Northwest's timber backlands… a book that seems destined to last."
—*The Oregonian*

"Heilman takes on big questions in humble prose… he tests assumptions, giving readers the opportunity to question and deliberate—to 'essay' their own trials—as well."
—Irene Wanner, *The Seattle Times*

"Overstory: Zero is a lovely, reminiscence-provoking book, one sure to be read with nods of recognition."
—Murray Morgan, *The News-Tribune*

$15.95 USD
From
Sylph Maid Books
P.O. Box 932
Myrtle Creek OR
97457
U.S.A.